A GENTLE AND LOWLY CHRISTMAS

∙∙∙

A MILDRED BUDGE FRIENDSHIP STORY

DAPHNE SIMPKINS

Quotidian Books

Montgomery, AL

Daphne Simpkins/Quotidian Books
Contact: QuotidianToday@gmail.com

A Gentle and Lowly Christmas/ Daphne Simpkins -- 1st ed.
ISBN 978-1-957435-10-7

Contents

1 Early Bird Christians 9

2 God Rest Ye Merry Gentlemen 13

3 Abide With Me 23

4 Christmas Fudge 27

5 Die Hard is a Christmas Movie 35

6 Come Thou Long Expected Jesus 43

7 O Come All Ye Faithful 51

8 A Bleak Midwinter 63

9 On Borrowed Time 69

10 Diamond Jake 75

11 Music on Christmas Eve 85

12 All Hands on Deck The Halls 95

13 Dixie is a Good Samaritan 101

14 Silent Night 107

15 Steev Loses Heart 113

16 O Little Town of Bethlehem 119

17 I'll Be Home for Christmas 127

18 Remember the Night 131

19 Going My Way 139

20 Calling Home at Christmas 147

21 Potluck for Christmas 151

22 Mildred's House on Christmas Eve 155

23 At Home on Christmas Eve 159

24 Dinner Next Year? 167

25 Mildred's Christmas Eve Ham Biscuits 169

26 And To All A Good Night 175

Bonus Excerpt Mildred Budge in Cloverdale 189

Books by Daphne Simpkins... 209

ABOUT Daphne Simpkins.. 210

*For my friends who love
a gentle and lowly Christmas*

Every day is a good day.

–Mildred Budge

1

EARLY BIRD CHRISTIANS

The powers that be had decided all of a sudden to have only one Christmas Eve service instead of two, and the time for that service was to be at 4 o'clock, not 6 o'clock.

There was a reason for the change to be made.

For most of the life of the Church on the Corner there had been two Christmas Eve services, but neither service was full now.

The split population in attendance caused the elders, whose formal name was the Guiding Light Session, to reconsider the extra work of two services on such a busy evening. After much praying and lots of discussion, they decided to host one Candlelight Service only on Christmas Eve at four o'clock.

The hope was that when people met for only one service, unity among the brethren would be nurtured in the Christmas spirit of good will toward all men—and from that simple hope, greater unity among the brethren would grow and be sustained throughout the new year.

But as always, when change was proposed, division happened first.

To meet the unhappy rumblings about the decision head-on, the Guiding Light Session decided to send out a survey to get some feedback after the fact.

The Guiding Light Session learned this from the survey.

The decision to have only one service on Christmas Eve severely split the church. Fifty-one percent of the people who had an opinion agreed vigorously that they LOVED the 4 PM service, stressing that word LOVED because they feared the survey would trigger a reversal, and they did not want to go to church at 6 o'clock.

Comments read like this:

It's a no-brainer if you ask me. Let's get church done on Christmas Eve so we can go home and start the fun. That is what Christmas Eve is for: family fun.

The other forty-nine percent voted differently, writing in ALL CAPS on the survey that they preferred a 6 PM service and that supper and Santa Claus could wait. The six o'clockers did not mention fun, but the dismissal of Santa Claus told that truth plainly. Fun was not on the agenda for the six o'clockers.

No one said out loud what many people who did not get asked what they preferred—somehow they did not get the survey and they were upset about that!-- that the 6 o'clockers were traditional church-goers, who had the *Book of Common Prayer* on their bedside tables and used it. The 4 PM people were Early Bird Christians, who saw their daily life as a long to-do list that they wanted to accomplish, checking off each item on the list day after day and certainly on Christmas Eve when getting that 4 PM service done was an accomplishment and a no-brainer.

The sudden change in the annual routine for Christmas Eve became almost instantly a kind of cautionary tale that led to the other bitter discussion of why a soda costs a dollar a can from the vending machine at the church, which was not prominently displayed. The vending machine was kept in a shadowy alcove with the lights turned low for the sake of the consciences of people who did not want the church to be seen as any kind of a marketplace.

No one could really justify coffee being free (tea, too), while sodas cost money.

The difference fueled the idea that there was an *us* and a *them*. There were church members who got to drink for free and church members who had to pay for what they wanted to drink. That is not unity in a church.

After the deadline for the return of the controversial surveys had passed, the discussion shifted to the sugar cookies that would be served at the Christmas Eve reception after the service.

Instantly, people were worried.

Because there was only one service, there was going to be a big crowd going after the cookies. They were very good cookies. People waited for the sugar cookies all year round. It was going to be a stampede! At four o'clock no one would have had supper. By the time the service ended at five o'clock, people would be hungry. People would want more than one cookie or even two cookies.

It was decided by everyone who knew how good those sugar cookies tasted that it would be best to get to the church to snag the best parking spot near the door by the main foyer that had the gigantic Christmas tree.

That entrance through the foyer had the strategically straightest route to the best pews at the front of the sanctuary, which is where you want to sit if you want to exit first after the Candlelight service and get to the reception room ahead of other people where the sugar cookies would be piled high on platters, but not for long.

The early bird with the seat in the sanctuary that was closest to the reception room would get the most sugar cookies.

2

GOD REST YE MERRY GENTLEMEN

There were two things about Kathryn Harris that most people knew without really knowing they knew it.

The former local tennis champ and current Ambassador of Love at the Church on the Corner had a great smile; and when Kathryn smiled in your direction, you felt better.

The second benefit that occurred from knowing Kathryn Harris, which people experienced but also did not talk about, was if you were a friend of Kathryn Harris's and lunched with her often, you began to lose weight.

There was nobody better at portion control when dining out than Kathryn; and when you were with her, you began to imitate the size of her portions too--painlessly.

If you ate with Kathryn often enough, you began to eat less and less; and before you had time to make a New Year's resolution or regret the failure of the one from the previous year, ten pounds fell off--painlessly. You never felt deprived or in a strain, and you never binged on potato chips or got up at midnight to raid the refrigerator. You simply lost weight; and if you routinely socialized with Kathrn, you kept it off.

Eating out with Kathryn was more effective than going to Weight Watchers or any other diet.

She did not get any credit for the blessings others enjoyed by eating out with her.

And she did not want it really.

Kathryn was generally too busy with church work to be aware of how many people wanted to be able to smile as she did or achieve and maintain her tennis champion figure.

A church worker bee, Kathryn had taken on much of the behind-the-scenes work for the 4 PM Candlelight Service.

For her ailing friend who usually oversaw the set-up of the Christmas tree, Kathryn Harris stepped in to make sure the tree was upright and in place for the congregation.

The annual church Christmas tree was supplied by David, one of the members of the church who had a Christmas tree farm. The tree David donated was always about four feet taller than he was—and David was tall.

Though no one had ever sent out a survey about the Christmas tree, one hundred percent of the people who attended the Church on the Corner liked a real live, very tall Christmas tree.

David chose the tree, delivered the tree, set up the tree, and then Kathryn organized the gals from the Berean Sunday school class to come and trim it. The ladies knew where the box of special decorations was stored, and they had that tree trimmed the week after Thanksgiving.

As a reward for their labor, they lunched on a platter of deli sandwiches from Chappy's. It was a small platter, and because Kathryn Harris was the hostess, everyone ate only one-half of a sandwich.

Her ministry did not stop there.

For her friend Fran, who was recovering from cancer and had lost her appetite for sweets, Kathryn had agreed to oversee the baking of the popular sugar cookies for the Christmas Eve service.

Immediately, Kathryn began to receive inquiries about just how many cookies there would be because, *you know, we've only got that one service and people are going to be hungry and there's going to be a rush.*

She fielded questions, like:

How many dozens are going to be baked?

Do you need extra money to buy the ingredients because I would give extra money to support making the cookies?

What are you going to do with the left-over cookies, if there are any?

A natural leader with a great respect for the validity of group-think, Kathryn smiled her way through the relentless interrogation about the sugar cookies. Then, she consulted every experienced cook in the congregation and asked for guesstimates of how many dozens of sugar cookies to make for the Christmas reception.

After five different women hit on the same number, Kathryn added six dozen to that projected total amount needed and made up a production flow chart for the cooks.

Without consultation with anyone, she made an important and radical executive decision.

Although people liked to imagine that the popular Christmas sugar cookies were baked in the church kitchen, to produce as many cookies as were needed, that plan simply was not feasible.

Some cookies would be made in the church kitchen.

Some other cookies would be made in the homes of volunteer cooks because there simply was not enough baking time the afternoon of Christmas Eve to rotate that many batches of cookie dough through the church oven.

Poppy, the girl who helped to write the church newsletter and was a budding journalist at the local college, caught up with Miss Kathryn in the ladies' room and asked her if she could have a copy of the sugar cookie recipe to print in the Christmas edition of the church newsletter. "People are afraid there won't be enough cookies and are worried that they might need to make some sugar cookies at home in order to, you know, not be disappointed in Christmas. The recipe is not a secret, is it?" Poppy asked, eyes squinting behind a pair of very narrow oval sunglasses that John Lennon had made popular years ago.

"As far as I know the cookie recipe is not a secret," Kathryn replied sunnily. "I just don't know the recipe off the top of my head. I will get back to you."

"When?" Poppy asked, her smile fading as Kathryn's grew.

"Toot de suite," Kathryn replied, once again sunnily.

"What does toot de suite mean exactly?" Poppy asked, her voice growing steely, for she had been taught what to do by her journalism professor if she encountered a hostile witness during an interview. Invade their personal space and ask more questions!

"I will email the recipe to you when I know exactly what it is," Kathryn replied, and left the ladies' room quickly, wondering if the young journalism major would chase after her.

She did not. And for that Kathryn was thankful. She found a quiet place in the church kitchen where she phoned Mildred Budge. Her good friend answered in French.

"Bonjour! Joyeux Noel!" Mildred said gaily.

"Bonjour, Millie," Kathryn replied. She was glad to hear the Christmas joy in Mildred's voice, and she smiled. "Have you got a minute?"

"Always. More if you need it," Mildred replied, studying her new outfit in the full-length mirror that she was planning to wear to the Christmas Eve service. She loved the way the silky cloth felt and the different bright colors she did not ordinarily wear. It was a blousy teal top and a full silver skirt. The holiday evening ensemble didn't exactly look like her, but it did feel like her. She smiled at the reflection and wondered if she could lose five pounds by Christmas Eve.

"Are you sure?" Kathryn asked, hearing distraction in her friend's voice. "I can call back later if you are busy."

Mildred came back to the moment, turning her back on her reflection and the prospect of spending Christmas Eve with Jake and her friends who were coming over after the service for a Potluck supper. "I am here, Katarina. What's on your mind?"

Kathryn ignored the sudden invention of a new nickname and got to the reason for her call.

"The newsletter girl wants the sugar cookie recipe, and I didn't want to bother Fran. I was planning to get it from her at the right time, only I don't know when the right time is these days. Do you know the recipe?"

"Of course," Mildred replied readily. "We have a traditional sugar cookie recipe in the church cookbook, but I don't think we have used it in years. Times change. Now, we just use any basic sugar cookie recipe; and to be honest with you, I think we have used that Betty Crocker mix off the grocery store shelf often. They sometimes put that mix on sale during this time of year. When it's on sale buy one, get one free, using the mix is cheaper than buying all the ingredients separately."

"A mix?" Kathryn repeated. "Are you sure?"

"Of course I am sure. There is nothing wrong with using a mix," Mildred assured her.

"I shall tell the truth then," Kathryn said, though she felt a tug of misgiving.

When you are raised on the tales of Southern belles and have read stories about princesses finding a prince, there is this tendency to want to romanticize life no matter how old you are. To say that they did not have a special Berean recipe for sugar cookies was the truth but, in Kathryn Harris's mind, a disappointing one.

Kathryn prayed on the matter and then wrote an announcement that answered the journalism student's question and which could be printed in the December newsletter.

Her message read like this:

"God rest ye merry gentlemen and gentlewomen. Tidings of comfort and joy to you and yours. Thanks be to God for an anonymous benefactor who has asked for the privilege of paying for all the cookie ingredients made for Christmas Eve. We are going to have plenty of cookies. Come to church Christmas Eve with a singing heart, and we will give you cookies to eat afterwards. A basic sugar cookie recipe is all we have traditionally used. You can find one in the church cookbook. Or, check with your good friend Betty Crocker. That mix of hers is church-lady friendly. We do have a secret ingredient for how we make the special Christmas sugar cookies. We make them with love. It is the Berean way."

That idea of a Cookie Benefactor created a big mystery, which was equivalent to the kind of romance that Kathryn believed made life better!

Conversations occurred near the church coffee pot and in the shadowy alcove where the vending machine purred:

Who could it be?
I bet it is that girl who sings in the choir who does not wear any other clothes under her choir robe.
How do you know that she doesn't wear any clothes?
I heard about it somewhere.
What is her name?
I don't remember her name.
Then it could be any woman up there singing in the choir loft wearing only a choir robe.

Oh, my.

It could be anybody.

Kathryn hid her responses to the cookie questions behind a wardrobe of smiles—all of them powerful because they were genuine. She enjoyed life and Christmas, and her enjoyment showed on her face.

Having decided that the cookie situation was under control, the people who liked to look ahead went on to their next worry, which was whether Steev, the preacher who spelled his name with two e's in the middle instead of the right way, was going to talk too long on Christmas Eve.

It was easy to worry that he would.

The young man was not married, had no excited children at home who were wondering what would be under the tree the next morning and no toys to assemble, so unless someone had a health emergency that meant the young minister needed to be at a sick person's bedside on Christmas Eve there was nothing that insisted Steev keep his Christmas Eve message short.

And....

The young preacher was still excited about the gospel. Steev could get really fired up on Sunday mornings.

People were nervous about how excited the young preacher might be about Christmas Eve.

They tried to disciple him.

Well-wishers and mentors said things like this to the new preacher:

"Looking forward to your short homily on Christmas Eve."

"Children enjoy a short homily, and there will be a lot of children getting restless in that hour-long service."

"A homily lasts twenty minutes. No more. That is what the word short means."

Everyone who talked to Steev emphasized the word *homily* instead of sermon.

But did the young preacher hear them?

3

ABIDE WITH ME

At three o'clock on Christmas Eve Mildred Budge was dressed and waiting for Jake Diamond to arrive and pick up her and Chase for the early evening service.

Her house was tidy and ready for company to join them after the service.

Two teenage boys who helped her through the year had come and blown all the leaves from her yard into fragrant piles on the street curb for the city to vacuum into their big machine.

The driveway had been power-washed with a cleanser that made Mildred think of Clorox, one of her favorite fragrances, but the boys had assured her that it wouldn't hurt her driveway.

The kitchen cabinets had been wiped down.

Paper plates and colorful cups were stacked near the jugs of ice tea and the Igloo cooler with extra ice.

And she had dispensed with worrying about any kind of dessert because everyone should have gotten at least one cookie, and when you have hot buttered biscuits and maple syrup nearby, do you need anything else sweet?

Besides, people would be bringing dishes, and someone would bring something sweet for the people who loved dessert.

Mildred closed her eyes and savored the moment. The smell of her large baked ham was redolent evoking memories of Christmas past.

She relished Christmas.

She loved the quiet and the noise, the lights and the shadows, the fragrance of evergreens, and the music. Always the music.

Mildred did not know why they didn't sing Christmas carols throughout the year, for deep inside her, she kept the joy of all that Christmas meant and could mean in her heart year-round. *O, come all ye faithful, joyful and triumphant. O come ye, o come ye to Bethlehem.*

In recent years the congregation's diminishing size had determined that two Christmas Eve services were not needed. Though surprised by the Guiding Light Session's decision to host only one service this year, Mildred adjusted immediately, believing that the Session was wrong and, at the same time, that it was none of her business to second-guess them. She had usually attended both services on Christmas Eve, but she could be satisfied with only one service this year, especially since so many friends were coming to her house afterwards.

She checked the back door to confirm that it was unlocked in case someone got to her bungalow in Cloverdale before she could return with Jake and Chase, a boy she was raising for parents who had abandoned him.

The boy seemed to be excited about Christmas too.

She was pleased, though disappointed that Janie, a new mother who was also living with her was not going to the service. Janie had been in a sour mood of her own for the whole afternoon but claimed her reason to stay home was because her Baby Sam was teething. That wasn't the whole truth. There was some unpleasantness about the church program for the evening service not being right, and now there wasn't one. Janie was being blamed for causing the trouble! Mildred did not want to know more. It was Christmas Eve, and trouble could wait.

Janie was moving about in her room with Baby Sam.

Chase was getting dressed in his room.

Mildred was listening for Jake to arrive and thinking about her new silvery skirt and how it would feel good to be riding in the classic Mercedes with Jake and Chase and being free of Janie's mood by simply leaving it behind.

She eyed the clock on the wall. She had a half hour to wait yet.

"The joy of the Lord is your strength," Mildred whispered. Her class had just finished a study of Nehemiah, and it was her keepsake verse from the study.

It was a new prayer proclamation, an amen to the truth that was ongoing, vital, and while transparent also mysteriously romantic and enticing.

"The joy of the Lord is your strength. The joy of the Lord is my strength."

The repetition of the words hallowed her heart, fed her soul, and cleansed her mind of worry as she opened her refrigerator and counted the cans of biscuits. Eight. Eight times eight is sixty-four. That would surely be enough biscuits.

She closed the refrigerator door and said the words again, "The joy of the Lord is my strength."

And it was.

4

CHRISTMAS FUDGE

Chase found Miss Mildred in the kitchen with her hand on the closed refrigerator door. He got right to the point.

"Why are we giving away all the fudge?" Chase asked. He was dressed in a green and red striped flannel shirt and wearing a pair of skinny jeans that had fit him a month ago. Now they were looking a smidge short. His sandy hair had been freshly cut, but it was sprouting here and there, making him look as if he was slightly electrified.

Mildred resisted the impulse to reach out and pat his wild hairs down.

The boy had been dropped off on her doorstep months ago and was growing stronger every day. He was asking more and more questions now and that was a good sign. Mildred Budge approved of curiosity.

"We are not giving away all of the fudge," Mildred replied at a pace where a child could process her answer.

She was becoming increasingly reminded of something she had once known very well. Children share a common bond with older people. Both age groups prefer a slower pace of communication. Children need a slower pace of taking in fresh information to process it. Older people have so much information stored inside of them that they, too, need a slower pace to integrate news into a great reservoir of stored history.

"I kept a pound of fudge for us," she explained one more time.

"Just a pound?" Jake asked, coming in through the back porch screen door. He was carrying a large cardboard box of Indian River fruit.

She smiled. She loved Indian River grapefruit. Oranges, too.

"A pound is a lot of candy," she said, wondering if Jake liked her new teal blouse and the silver skirt.

Jake's gaze warmed when he looked at Mildred. "I'm going to put the box of fruit by the front door for people to help themselves as they leave."

She nodded, as his hand reached out and patted her shoulder. *Nice blouse. Pretty color.*

His eyes smiled. "I guess we can always make more fudge if we have an emergency, or even eat an orange," Jake teased. "I have another box out in the car. When we come home, I'll put that box on the back porch for people who leave that way. The Boy Scouts were selling the fruit for a fundraiser."

Mildred nodded. She remembered when her family used to buy the fruit each year, but as time passed she had lost track of the Boy Scouts, and a large box of oranges and grapefruits was simply too much fruit for her.

"There is no limit on how much fudge we make. If we have sugar, cocoa, milk, butter, and vanilla extract we can make fudge."

"Do we have all that?" Chase asked, concerned. They had given away a great deal of the fudge. This next trip to take some to Fran and Winston would be the last.

"Always," Mildred replied.

It was true that Mildred Budge could make chocolate fudge any day of the week any week of the year, but she usually waited until the Christmas season between Thanksgiving and December 25. She had already made eight batches because many of her friends requested it. She did not consider making candy a hardship. There might be even another fudge-making day before New Year's to stretch out the Christmas season. It had been an especially sweet season this year.

Chase closed his eyes briefly. She saw him swallow what he was thinking.

"Do not worry. We will not be long at Fran's and Winston's. We are just going to drop off the fudge and then head to church."

Mildred did not add: Where my friends from the Berean Sunday school class are still baking the sugar cookies for the holiday reception.

Mildred felt a tug of longing to be with the other church ladies in the church kitchen cooking and laughing. Some of the best times she had known were in the church kitchen with her good friends cooking. Sometimes it was baking cookies. Sometimes it was making casseroles to store up in the big deep freezer from which people who needed a quick dish to take to an ailing or recovering friend could help themselves.

Stocking the freezer with take-along casseroles anyone could grab and go with was one of the best decisions the church ladies had ever made. Add a tin foil pan of Sister Schubert yeast rolls and a quart of soup or a poppyseed casserole, and the person who was trapped at the house was glad to see you. Add a fresh loaf of bread, a jug of milk, a can of coffee (with a package of filters), and sometimes a six-pack of toilet paper rolls, and you were truly ministering to the poor in spirit—that is, the homebound.

"How many cookies can we eat?" Chase asked. He had heard about the sugar cookies. The other children from his Sunday school class had told him they were lip-smacking good.

"Yeah, how many cookies can we eat?" Jake teased. His green brown eyes were merry with amusement. "Can we ruin our supper?"

"I think you can eat a ham biscuit just fine after you eat your share of cookies."

"How many cookies is my share?" Chase pressed.

"Two," she said simply. "Or three."

"Four?" Chase pressed.

"You can have mine," she agreed. "Which means you can have four."

By now the kitchen counter at church would be laden with platters covered in white paper doilies. The ladies would be almost finished with the baking. The bowls for mixing would be soaking. Someone would wash them for the last time before night's end and turn them upside down to dry on the long bright yellow absorbent cloth that stretched out three feet on the biggest counter. Just before making the large coffee urn Sunday morning, whoever showed up to do that would put away the big bowls right where they belonged. A lot of people at the Church on the Corner knew where that was.

"Are we ready?" Mildred asked. She stopped for a moment to listen for Janie to come out and say good-bye, 'can I do anything for you while you are gone?' but the girl was moodily behind her closed door.

"We are ready," Jake said, leading the way.

Wordlessly, they left through the back door of Mildred's bungalow and walked around the house to the classic green Mercedes that Mildred had signed over to Jake when she bought it as part of a house that came with everything in it: lock, stock, barrel, and a classic car.

He and Chase had brought the car back to life and cleaned it out and waxed it. The car gleamed in the late afternoon sunlight.

They all took their regular seats. Chase was in the back, and Mildred and Jake were in the front. Jake drove.

There was no hint of a new car smell. But there was the faintest lingering scent of a pipe having been smoked inside the classic car long, long ago. Way back when, Mildred's dad had from time to time smoked a pipe. She liked the nudge of that memory.

The leather interior had been waxed. The old-fashioned radio remained off. Each person's belt stayed exactly as it had been used before and released—no struggling to tighten or loosen it again.

It was a beautiful time of day, and the air had some cold bite to it. There was no sign of rain. As Jake eased the car out of the driveway, Mildred smiled at the four-foot angel blowing a trumpet in her front yard. She liked that angel. But she liked all kinds of decorations, not worrying so much about reconciling the myth of Santa Claus and his elves to the eternal story of Bethlehem upon which she had built the house called her life. Having taught children for twenty-five years, Miss Budge still simply found the characters of childhood stories amusing.

As they drove, she smiled at all the holiday decorations along the route. No matter what their owners may have been trying to say about Christmas, something that all her neighbors had in common was a celebratory spirit: they greeted the season with lights and outdoor decorations. White, round snowmen stood beside three wise men and a manger. In one yard, the big green Grinch was taller than the tilting Santa Claus. Occasionally, there were even skeletons and ghosts that had been put up at Halloween and not taken down yet.

"Do you see that angel, Chase?" Jake asked.

In the backseat, the boy appeared to be passive, resigned to giving away the fudge.

As they turned toward Winston's house where Fran and her new husband were now living while she got well, Chase said, "I like our angel better."

"I do, too," Jake interjected. "I say we get another angel for next year and have two. We can add an angel every year until we have a choir of them in the front yard for Christmas," Jake said.

"Have you ever seen a real angel?" Chase asked.

"A few times," Jake said, easily.

Mildred listened carefully. Intimacies of life were often shared best this way, with a curious child who did not try to argue you out of what you have decided was a real experience.

"What do angels look like?" Chase asked, fixing his gaze on Jake now.

The blown up Grinches, reindeer, angels, Santas, and elves in the yards of people they were driving by were now ignored.

"Angels going about their business here on the planet Earth don't all look the same," Jake answered honestly. "And I can only tell you about a couple of angel possibilities, because there is no way to be sure you have seen one. Or two."

His hands gripped the leather-covered steering wheel. The classic car suited Jake. It suited Mildred, too. She admired how the light landed on the planes of his face. He had good teeth. And he was wearing a red necktie with an A on it for the football team he supported, but it worked for Christmas, too.

"Or three?" Chase pressed. The boy loved Jake, was closer to him now in ways that he wasn't with Mildred. That suited her too. When you have taught school for twenty-five years, you understand that children need more than one adult to trust—to love.

"To be honest with you, I have lost count," Jake admitted.

"Four?" Chase pressed.

"Maybe," Jake replied with an agreeable shrug.

"Five?" Chase asked.

As they steered into Fran's and Winston's driveway, Jake waited until he had turned off the engine to answer the question. "Goodness and mercy will follow you all the days of your life, and angels come and go all the time making sure that happens. You can believe the Bible."

Mildred relaxed in the soft shadows of the car and encroaching twilight. She believed that too. She was comfortable with Goodness and Mercy being the names of angels.

"The next time you think you see an angel even if you aren't sure, will you tell me?" Chase asked, leaning forward, straining against his seat belt. His chin almost rested on the front seat, and he had his eyes on Jake.

"Of course," Jake promised. "You will be the first person I tell," Jake promised.

But then he flashed him a grin and said, "But you make sure that you do the same for me."

5

DIE HARD IS A CHRISTMAS MOVIE

Fran must have heard the car roll up into the driveway or been watching for them because she opened the front door before they reached it.

Standing behind her in the dark was her husband Winston, a tall, quiet man who liked taxing physical work but was comfortable being still. The house was dark, not a piece of red ribbon hanging anywhere or a Christmas light shining on the front porch.

'I should have brought a wreath for the door,' Mildred thought. And just that quickly she dismissed the idea and the guilt. When people are persevering through an illness, they can accept certain kinds of help but maybe not a wreath or even a front-yard angel blowing a trumpet.

"Mildred," Winston said. "You look nice."

Fran concurred in a tense, bright voice. "I had forgotten about that skirt."

Mildred grabbed the sides of the skirt and stretched it out to display the fullness.

The silver swirling skirt reached Mildred's ankles, negating the need to wear hose, and hiding broken veins that still surprised her. 'How did that happen? I am just walking, and yet, there are places on my legs that look as if I have been injured.' The changes in your body that seemed to occur while you were not watching and then suddenly discovered were still a surprise though they had been happening all her life. Mildred wondered what Fran thought of her own body going through the treatment for cancer.

Jake reached for Mildred's hand. She let go of the skirt and stepped closer to him.

Fran was wearing loose-fitting clothes, the kind of jersey pants and sweatshirt that she had forbidden Mildred Budge to ever wear.

Until her illness and the treatment for it, Fran had always declared, "Stretch pants do not do a thing for you. Not a thing. And, if you have any problems you would like to disguise, you cannot hide anything in stretch pants."

That had been Fran's rule, and she was breaking it on Christmas Eve. Fran was wearing stretchy clothes that were loose on her,   hiding the truth that she was thinner than she needed to be. She had grown tired of people remarking upon her weight loss and encouraging her to eat. Bullying her about food is how Fran experienced it. So, she had bought stretchy, loose clothes that hid how much weight she had lost.

"Chase, you look very spiffy," Fran said, her voice growing intimate and sincere. She leaned over, trying to make eye contact with Chase.

Fran's breath was sour, but she did not know it. Chase stepped back and moved toward Jake, who was closer.

Mildred filed away the boy's reaction, wondering if the sight of someone recovering from an illness made him uncomfortable. Mildred did not remember a time growing up when she did not know someone chronically ill. Her parents had been veteran visitors of ill people and had taken her with them. And they had never gone empty-handed. Her mother's signature best-wishes-to-you-and-yours-get-well soon take-along dish was Apricot Nectar cake. Mildred had not tasted that cake since her mother had died, but she suddenly wished she were holding one instead of the fudge. Apricot Nectar cake was unusual and often irresistible to people who have lost their appetite.

The memories returned.

Caregivers, who were so eager for their patient to eat a little something, called with gratitude for the special cake and report the small but important improvements in their patient eating:

"She nibbles on it frequently."

"He got up the other night and cut himself a piece of that cake."

"He is actually eating it—even the crumbs. How do you make the glaze? He is actually licking his fingers!"

"We are grateful for every bite she takes. What's the recipe?"

"Are you coming inside?" Winston asked, his hand on the door and pulling it back.

Jake smiled, but he did not answer. Chase looked over his shoulder at the parked car. Jake placed a steadying hand on the boy's shoulder. Chase leaned into him.

"Here's some fudge," Chase declared suddenly, holding out the plastic container.

It was a medium-size plastic disposable box with blue snowflakes printed on the base and with a red plastic seal. There were about twelve pieces of fudge in it--plenty for two people.

Winston reached for the box of candy while Fran tried to smile as if she were glad they had brought some more. But the automatic move of her hand to cover her mouth told the real story. Fran presently lived with a kind of chronic nausea and the thought of swallowing food was like a punch in the gut. This condition was extreme, but not unusual. Fran had always talked about food with more appetite than she really felt for it.

"I love Christmas Eve at church," Fran confessed to cover the moment of discomfort. "The Christmas tree in the foyer always smells so fresh. The ladies will have finished baking the cookies by now. I did so love the smell of warm cookies baking in the oven. Win, I will make you some as...." Fran began and then stopped herself. She had decided not to make plans, to make no promises she did not know she could keep. She was just going to get through Christmas and face the New Year, whatever it would bring.

"There will be time for everything," Winston promised. He took a step back, away from Mildred and Chase and the night and into the darkened enclosed life of his wife recovering from an illness and adjustment to married life that had not really happened for either of the newlyweds yet.

"You folks go on. Eat a cookie for me, Chase. Eat two! We are fine," Winston encouraged.

It was a brave and generous send-off.

'Winston was a man worthy of her best friend,' Mildred thought.

"Thanks, Millie. We will have some fudge later. My girl wants to watch….what was the name of that movie you wanted to watch?"

Fran looked down at her feet. Fran had no more interest in watching a movie than she did in eating fudge. Still, she tried to remember. *What had she said*? She knew the list of perennial favorites that were supposed to keep you company during the holidays. *Meet Me in St. Louis. The Bishop's Wife. Holiday Affair. Holiday Inn.* She guessed at an answer. "*White Christmas*?"

"Listen to her. I told her *Die Hard* was a Christmas movie, but she has not seen it. I have about talked her into watching *Die Hard* for the first time," Winston boasted.

He was trying very hard.

"*Die Hard* is pretty good, Fran," Jake agreed. "In fact, if I didn't already have plans I would come on in there, throw some chili together, and we would all watch it."

"Chili?" Winston brightened.

Winston was eating what Fran was eating, and it was mostly bland. There had been a lot of chicken soup, more than one soupy chicken casserole made with unsalted pasta, and Belle's signature dish that he was trying to forget: tuna fish casserole.

"Chili sounds good. How does chili sound to you, Fran?" Winston asked hopefully.

Fran pulled her shoulders back and answered, "We have some chili in the freezer." Her lips were dry, but she tried to stretch them into a smile. "Somebody brought it to us."

"*Die Hard*. Chili, then fudge," Winston said, waking up to the moment. He smiled authentically for the first time and looked like he wanted to hold the door wide open and say, 'I am sure there will be plenty. Come on in!' Winston was shy, but he was hospitable.

Fran felt the change in her husband. Her expression softened. She turned slightly, and looked the way she had at their wedding when the preacher asked all the questions that ended with "I do." The words dwelled inside of her, but now her vows of love felt not like hope but heartbreak.

"Y'all better get a move on. We will be there with you next year. I like those sugar cookies," Winston said. "Every year they taste the same, but every year they kind of also tasted different. But they were always good—those cookies. All those years, when I was eating them I did not know you two gals were helping to make them."

Fran opened her mouth to say, 'I will make you some sugar cookies right now,' but she stopped herself. They had been standing in the doorway for less than five minutes, and she needed to sit down already.

To sit down on that couch in the other room that was not her couch and try to get well in a living room that was not her own living room and watch a TV that was not her TV was challenging. Fran did not feel at home in Winston's house yet, and she did not feel at home in her own body, which was worse. She had become discombobulated by her breast cancer diagnoses right after her marriage, and the newlyweds had not been able to resolve the problem of having two houses between them yet. Fran did not say the words out loud, but her quandary was that if she was going to die sooner rather than later, she did not want Winston stuck in her house where he would feel as uncomfortable after losing her as she did in his house while they were waiting to see what would happen next in her body.

"It is your first time to eat the famous sugar cookies. Eat some cookies for me, Chase," Winston repeated. "Now you kids go on. Otherwise, you will not get a good parking spot. This is no time to be late. The early bird gets the best parking spot. Y'all go on. We have got a special evening planned, and we are fine. Just fine," he promised, putting a protective arm around his bride's shoulder.

Fran tilted her head toward him and closed her eyes. He could have scooped her up and carried her to the couch if it was necessary, but she held herself upright, tenuous though it was.

"*Die Hard,* chili and fudge," Fran said, brightly, and she shivered. "Merry Christmas."

The others might believe her, but Mildred Budge heard the difference. "Merry Christmas!"

"Same to you," Winston said. "Chase, remember to eat a cookie for me."

Winston watched them as they walked back to the car, not telling a soul that he loved Christmas Eve. It was his favorite night of the year. Winston loved the music, the quiet times during the evening, and the comforting ease of a half-filled sanctuary where you could stretch out in the pew and had enough space around you to let your mind roam. Your memories become surprisingly good company. Winston liked the lullaby tempo of old, old carols, the familiar hominess of a preacher telling the story of a Christ child being born, while your mind went back in time visiting the scenes of Christmas past that revealed themselves to you in the present moment with a kind of nurturing hope that murmured reassuringly: "All is well. And all will be well."

Winston closed the door. Quietly. And before they reached the car, he had flipped off the outside porch light. It was dark then—the only house on the block that had no hint of Christmas from color or lights.

Mildred Budge swallowed hard and turned toward the old Mercedes.

Jake came alongside Mildred and gripped her elbow in the old-fashioned way that men used to escort women from here to there. She absorbed the comfort of his steadying strength and wondered how she had lived so long without him.

6

COME THOU LONG EXPECTED JESUS

"I gotta go. Gonna preach tonight. Brother Joe is talked out," Sam declared to Belle, his wife, who was accustomed to such announcements and knew how to hear them. Her husband often thought he was going to preach because the regular preacher was preached out.

Belle studied Sam affectionately.

Sam had dressed himself in an old pair of black slacks that had fit him twenty pounds ago, and he was wearing a shirt with a collar. His brown leather belt did not match his black slacks and was cinched as tightly as it could go.

Sam had a new pair of smaller dress pants wrapped and waiting for him under the small Christmas tree. When she saw how her husband looked, Belle realized she should have given them to Sam already so he could wear the new smaller pants tonight. She simply had not thought of that idea. It had been so long since Belle had seen her husband take an interest in dressing up even a little bit that she almost fell to her knees and cried with what could be called a kind of Christmas joy that she was just learning about during this season of Alzheimer's and Christmas.

Just the hint that her old sweetheart remembered who he was caused her to feel like there was hope after all. And there was not. Not really. Not the kind of hope that people associate with progress or a tidy, happy ending. Sam had dementia, and his awareness of who he was and what was going on waxed and waned in ways that defied any strategy of explanation that medical professionals provided as if what they said was absolute truth. It was not. Still, Belle did not feel hopeless. She did not have a proper noun or adjective to describe this growing relationship with her husband who was in such a state of psychological restlessness. It was love, and it was still a growing love.

While Belle was studying him, Sam changed just that fast. He flapped his arms excitedly. "Let's hit the road, Jack," he urged. "Waste not, want not."

Time. Waste no time, want no time.

Sam could still draw out a cliché from the well of his very deep memory bank. Remarkably, when Belle heard Sam use old-timey phrases she took the time to dissect them. It was amazing how limited the human vocabulary is to tell the truth of what is happening. 'We make do with so little in our vocabulary,' she thought. 'Only the Bible gets to the truth—right to it.'

"God is love," she said aloud to her husband.

He eyed her quizzically. "Brother Joe is plumb tuckered," he said. "Plucked like a chicken."

Brother Joe, the former minister, had been tired and had left long ago. He had been replaced by substitutes for a while and most recently by the hiring of a full-time young minister.

The new preacher who had replaced Joe was Steev, and he was young and full of vim and vigor. 'Now, he has got me doing it,' Belle thought. 'I am thinking in cliches. What is vim anyway?' It had been so long since Belle Deerborn had experienced vigor, she did not even try to think of what it meant.

"Hustle up, buttercup. I will leave without you, girleo," Sam declared, heading to the front door. He stood there, his hand on the doorknob, unable to twist it sufficiently to open the door.

"First things first," he said, his hand dropping to his side. He was giving up more and more often. She did not want him to do that.

'Struggle on,' she thought, reaching past him to grip the doorknob.

It was stiff, not easy to turn. And as Belle twisted the knob she leaned closer to her husband and absorbed the heat and memory of him. Instinctively, she tried to kiss him, but Sam backed up.

"I will have you know I am a married man," Sam declared, holding up a hand.

Belle smiled faintly, by will as much as anything else. She opened the door and stepped back so he could leave. "You are a faithful married man. I beg your pardon," she said.

"First things first," he said, exiting ahead of her. He left his wife un-kissed and reproved.

It had been a while since her old husband had kissed her. Belle could not say how long. Later tonight when he was asleep, she would kiss him on the top of his head when he could not mistake her for someone else or interpret the move as an act of aggression. She had even kissed the tops of his feet when tucking him in and hoped in spite of his condition he would know deep inside himself that she loved him like that—from head to toe.

She prayed for him that way, too—from head to toe. Coming and going, Sam could so easily get into trouble.

"Keep your angels close," Belle prayed, as she watched her husband aim himself toward the car, squinting at it as if it were some kind of flying saucer that had landed in their driveway.

"Let goodness and mercy follow him all the days of his sacred life," she sighed.

It was not the first time she had prayed the goodness and mercy prayer.

Sam jiggled the car handle on the passenger side—where he remembered somehow that he sat now. It was locked. Belle pressed the button on the car key remote.

Eureka! Magic happened.

The door unlocked. Sam smiled.

"Where have you been?" he asked, looking over the top of the car. He would try the door handle again in a moment or so.

"Oh, here and there," Belle said.

And now, first things first. It was a big job to keep up with what should be first when the facts kept changing.

'What should be first on Christmas Eve?' Belle wondered.

She closed her eyes and waited for the knowledge to come to her; but when it did, she alone knew what it meant, but that did not mean she was wrong. 'Abide with me in the sacred moment—this moment. Breathe in the holiness of my love and breathe it out as an amen.' And then the most mysterious refrain began: 'I will help you walk on water if you want to do that. Come to me. First things first.'

Was that her idea, or did it come from somewhere else? There was absolutely no one to ask, and no way to confirm the idea as fact.

Since old Al, short for Alzheimer's, had moved in with them, Belle craved a good fact, but they existed in a different place in her value system. Facts were like inadequate words that barely told the truth. These days, facts were nebulous things based on human perception and memory. Both were intrinsically vulnerable to distortion. And as Belle reminded herself of that, she said to herself, and she talked to herself a lot, "And that's a fact."

And she laughed.

First things first. She had to get them both to church for the four o'clock service, which meant leaving at three o'clock. You never knew how long it would take to go from here to there.

"I do not have all day, bumblebee buzzing all over the place. I can hear you thinking," Sam declared. "Where are my sermon notes?"

"Everything you need is in the car," Belle replied easily.

"Well, all right then. Let's go."

"Keep us in perfect peace," she prayed, waiting to see if Sam could get himself into the car. *First things first.*

"Where is my sermon?" he demanded suddenly.

"Everything you need is already in the car," Belle said.

"Well, why didn't you say so?" Sam complained.

Sam wrenched open the door then, kicking at the side of the frame of the car with one foot as if he blamed it for being contrary, and then, once he got over that tiff, her old husband—a man she used to think of as her lover—dropped to a kind of squat, turned around, aimed his behind into the car, and then folded himself into the seat.

"Hallelujah!" Belle said, taking her place behind the steering wheel.

"I don't know what I am gonna do with you. It is the change of life, isn't it? You just keep changing, and you keep changing everything. It is hard to keep up. And I guess I can't hold it against you because you can't help being you."

"I do keep changing," Belle agreed. "You are right about that."

"It is about time you said so. I have waited a while to hear you say those words."

"I will try to do better," Belle replied. "Let's go see our friends."

"Oh, will they be there?" Sam asked, turning his head and staring at her in the car.

And before she could answer he asked another question, "Are you getting fat?"

Belle's hands gripped the steering wheel as she backed out of the driveway wearing the best outfit she now owned, an ensemble she had chosen from the closet of a dead woman's house that Mildred had bought to rent out. What a bonanza—a real Christmas avalanche of gifts. Mildred had invited Belle to come over and pick out whatever she wanted from that dear lady's closet.

Belle was not the only Berean invited to shop a dead woman's closet. "Just take what you want. And take your time too."

There was not a sentence Belle currently liked more than the unction: "Take your time."

She had taken her time in that woman's closet. And while there, Belle had enjoyed her first taste of Christmas, which was the unexpected boon of free dressy clothes she never would have bought for herself. She was now wearing her favorite: a dress that was the color of plums. The hem of the dress was trimmed in small images of silver bells, the kind that hang on a sleigh, and that is what Belle thought of when she saw them.

"Cause you look pretty fat," Sam said.

"You are right about that too. I am getting fat," Belle agreed easily. "But it is okay. You like me this way."

Sam grinned broadly and reached across the car and gripped her right thigh solidly. "You betcha, short stuff. You've got it going on."

"I do," Belle replied, and though it was a common response to a common refrain that had built up between the older married couple through the years, it was really an affirmation of her wedding vow. In a way that defied logic, saying the words "I do" strengthened the wife of a husband with dementia.

7

O COME ALL YE FAITHFUL

Liz Luckie did not like riding in Mark's station wagon. "It smells like manure!"

A vintage plant man in the spring and summer, Mark Gardiner did use manure. He tried to air out his station wagon, but nothing worked. It wasn't a problem for him, but Liz Luckie was repulsed by the aromas associated with a man who worked outdoors. She preferred Chanel #5.

And no matter how often Mark vacuumed it out and wiped down the interior with those waxy cloths that are supposed to leave behind the smell of real leather, even that effort did not solve the problem for Liz.

The interior of Mark's working man's station wagon did not smell good enough and was not clean enough for someone who liked to wear fur coats, fur-trimmed cloth coats, fur stoles, and most often when the occasion was a dressy affair, black velvet high heel shoes with bright rhinestone buckles.

Mark had not expected Liz to be attracted to the imitation sparkle of rhinestones, because Liz Luckie loved diamonds. But his lady liked rhinestone buckles too, clipped on the tops of dressy, evening shoes, Mark learned over time. And she had more than one pair of rhinestone buckles for different types of shoes.

One time residual grit from Mark's wagon clung to Liz's black velvet shoes, reminding the rich widow that her newest beau, and potentially husband number five, was a working man.

A working man could not afford Liz Luckie. And Mark Gardiner, in his current situation, which was barely scraping by, could not easily afford to disagree with her.

So, when Liz off-handedly told Mark that she was going to pick him up in her better car and drive them to the Candlelight Service on Christmas Eve, Mark did not offer to clean out the station wagon or get it washed fresh. He just said, "Yes, Liz."

Mark was learning that saying yes to Liz Luckie was the secret to getting along with her.

Standing at his front window, he was watching for Liz to arrive, hoping that having pressed his own jacket and shirt and chosen the necktie with the least fraying would be enough to convince her that his working man's station wagon was just like any other tool—not a commentary on him and his taste or her taste in men. At heart and in his more illustrious past, Mark Gardiner was a *GQ* man, someone who could still be on the cover of *Esquire* if he had the right clothes.

Once upon a time during his days as an actor, he had looked that good. Now, he was trying to stand in good lighting when he wore his older classic clothes and hoped that would be enough.

It was a strain.

Liz's upscale new model car turned the corner at the base of that sloping curve that he always took slowly when he was driving because the tail-end of his station wagon often slammed into the bumpy parts of that very old street. Liz did not worry about that. She could have her car repaired or buy another new one. So, she drove fast and turned sharply, speeding up just when he would have eased up on the gas.

"She almost scares me," Mark whispered to himself. "Driving like that, she could kill us both."

Mark repressed that fear, as Liz lurched onto his driveway, coming up the curving incline to align with an abrupt halt alongside his front door. He saw her high-powered car trembling and knew she had not put it in Park. Liz was holding down the brake with that rhinestone-buckled foot while the engine pulsed in his driveway, and she did not want to wait long. He could not see her hands from where he stood, but Mark knew from experience that her fingers would be strumming the steering wheel impatiently.

Mark moved quickly, tugging his big heavy front door closed behind him as he prepared a smile to greet her.

But Liz did not see the smile. She had flipped down the car visor to check her make-up. It had been a whole twenty minutes since she had left her house over in East Montgomery, and the gloss and color she assiduously applied might have faded in that amount of time. Using her forefinger, Liz touched the corners of her eyes, smoothed her eyebrows, and then daubed at the corner of each side of her mouth to remove any caked lip color there.

She did not lean over to help push open the car door. In fact, the passenger door was not even unlocked. Liz let her Christmas Eve date tug unsuccessfully on the car door handle a couple of times before she allowed herself to realize that the lock was keeping him out. That is when Mark realized that Liz Luckie had an innate instinct for this sort of gamesmanship.

Liz pushed the visor back up first. The light went out. Only then did she move her hand to unlock the door for him.

Finally, he heard the reassuring click of the car door unlock, and making his face smile again in greeting because she had not seen the first one, he said, "Hello, Beautiful."

Mark arched himself across the front seat for a hello kiss. Liz tilted her cheek in his direction. He landed an awkward peck, an unfortunate beginning.

It was still light enough outside that she could see his eyes, and he tried to make them smile, too, but it was hard. His head hurt—he was hungry-- and a back tooth was aching. No, it was more like the root of a tooth. The working man in Liz's posh car could foresee a root canal in his near future—one he could not afford.

"You look nice," he said, situating himself in the passenger seat. There was not enough floor room for his long legs.

"So do you," she said, scrutinizing his appearance. She had seen his outfit many times. He had only three jackets, and he was wearing his best one. Brooks Brothers. A classic Navy blazer that had known better days.

His khaki trousers were presentable, though out of season. He should have worn navy, but those pants were dirty, and he did not have the money to get them dry-cleaned. All his slacks were looser than before, and he had the awful suspicion that he was flattening out in the back the way old men do. Jokes were made about older men's flat behinds; and if his loose pants were any indication, he was already there. He was too old to care, too mature to bemoan the loss for he knew it was vanity, but he did anyway. His Brooks Brothers jacket was his only hope at disguise. It was so old—a classic that was cut differently than more modern jackets. The Brooks Brothers jacket hung longer in the back, and he hoped it covered his derriere deficiencies.

"We are going to get there plenty early," Liz said, steering them down the steep driveway just as he was fastening his seatbelt. "It is every man for herself," she said, incongruously.

He wanted to mutter, "himself," but he did not dare.

They both braced for the resounding bump of the car's tail-end when they reached the street.

'It is just a sound,' Mark promised himself.

Still, Liz grimaced.

"Are you sure about afterwards?" he asked to distract her from thinking too long about the inconvenience of where he lived.

"What did you say?" Liz replied sharply.

"Mildred's. Are you sure we are invited to Mildred's?"

"Of course, we are invited," Liz sniffed. "Millie and I go way back. I am invited every year though this is the first time she is not cooking the whole buffet supper," Liz said as she steered them across the cobblestone street. They bounced.

"This street will give your shocks a work out," Mark commented, hoping to make a joke of it.

"How much longer are you going to live in this no-man's land?" Liz asked irritably. Her diamond bracelet glittered under the car light.

'It was worth about four grand,' Mark estimated.

"Bloom where you are planted," he said, automatically. It was a gardener's joke, but Liz did not like to remember that he worked outdoors in the spring and summer in the vintage plant industry to supplement his social security check. He had no other retirement income. For most of his working life Mark had been in the entertainment industry, starting out as an actor, finding more work in radio, and later, much later, doing voice-overs for commercials.

When the retired actor had first moved to Montgomery, he had thought he could break into that industry here, but the advertising agencies already had their talent on board. They took one look at him, decided he was a has-been or over the hill, and did not wait to hear him give his spiel or even ask for his voice-over audio file or a resume. Just thinking about it made Mark tighten his necktie and then check both of his gold-plated cufflinks. He made his best money from the vintage plant business. But that market dried up during the fall and winter months. By the time spring and summer rolled around, he had to work up another list of potential clients because they seemed to evaporate between seasons. Or they stopped answering their telephone.

The vintage plant landscape business was always changing. Finding new clients was not as easy as connecting with Mildred Budge had been. Estate sales were good hunting grounds, but regulars attended them. He knew most of the regulars now. And they knew him. He knew he needed to move on to new hunting grounds, but he did not know where to go.

"I do not like your furniture. It is so dark and heavy," Liz announced suddenly as her thoughts wondered to other complaints she had about his house and the location of it. Her thoughts often drifted to this familiar complaint.

Mark knew that he was supposed to do something about her declaration, but he did not know how he could. He could not afford to buy new furniture, and he could not downsize and move to a better part of town.

He had no money saved, no relatives who would be glad to see him and give him room and board, and no idea about what else he could do. Old actors were like old horses—put out to pasture and forgotten. And then they died.

Stealing a glance in the driver's direction, Mark tried to imagine what it would be like to live out his days with Liz Luckie, who was always dressed to the nines and who was eager to make an entrance everywhere she went while, over time, he had more and more often desired to slip in and out of places unseen. If people looked at him too closely they would see in his older clothes that he was a present-day failure however glamourous his short-lived, long ago Hollywood past had been.

"We do not have to stay long at Mildred's. We will just put in an appearance. Eat a little something, and then we can do what we want to do," Liz declared.

Mark had no idea what Liz wanted to do, and he had nothing to offer her as refreshments at his house. He felt inadequate with Liz, and he was tired.

Mildred Budge had never made him feel like a failure and even when things had gone wrong between them she had always greeted him afterwards with something he could not name until he remembered the word that told the truth about her and which just remembering made his mouth go dry with longing: kindness.

The experience of kindness is like drinking water during a drought when you are so very thirsty. Mark licked his lips, thinking about Mildred Budge and her cooking and her ice tea and her peacefulness that welcomed others into a sphere of living that seemed foreign but natural, like you always hoped there was a place like that somewhere. It was hard to believe in kindness really, and somehow after you grow up and learn that fairy tales are only fairy tales and that there is no Santa Claus, you begin to dismiss ideas that there is such a thing as good will to others, but there was. Is. Mark Gardiner had experienced it.

Peace and kindness are real. You just have to find them in the people who know what they are and will share them with you.

"Are you all right?" Liz asked. "What are you doing with your mouth?"

Mitch had licked his lips again and then moved his tongue to find that tooth in the back that was throbbing. Maybe he would not need a root canal, which would surely cost more. Maybe he could just get it pulled. Thank God, the aching tooth was in the back where you could not see it. There was some kind of dental clinic in town somewhere that pulled teeth for free for poor people, but he did not know whom to ask about the location. To ask that question was to tell others the truth: I cannot afford to go to the dentist. Mark Gardiner could not afford for Liz Luckie to know that about him.

"Just thinking. Christmas Eve takes you back," Mark said, deflecting.

"I don't believe in looking back," Liz said sharply. "I do not believe in living on Memory Lane," Liz warned, turning onto the street that would take them almost directly to the church.

And though he was uncomfortable as her passenger, Mark admired that about her. 'Liz Luckie drove like a man.' Well, that was a sexist thought, and he knew better than to say something like that out loud, but really, Liz Luckie drove like a man—like a man who can drive.

"I do not like this time for the church service. This Podunk town with its small-town ways. Potluck suppers. Potluck! I hate the word potluck. It reminds me of that expression that I can barely make myself say."

"Then don't say it," Mark advised. His stomach grumbled. It had been a long time since he had eaten a slice of toast for breakfast, and he had not eaten any lunch. He did not have any food in his house to speak of. Potluck was a golden idea for him. A tableful of food sounded like Christmas to him. If he could eat enough at Mildred's, he would not miss breakfast so badly the next day.

"Do you know that some of the women in the church make something called a Dump Cake?"

"Is that like a pineapple upside-down cake?" he asked, trying to decipher the term as he wondered what kind of food Mildred would have. It did not matter. He would eat anything.

"Now why would you ask that?" Liz asked irritably. "And why would it matter? A dump cake is a dump cake is a dump cake. I cannot fathom why anyone would make and then serve something called a dump cake."

"Because they dump out a pineapple upside-down cake so that the bottom is up. Undumped."

He should not have said anything. Almost immediately, Mark felt a disastrous change in Liz's attitude toward him. Her foot came off the accelerator, and the fancy car slowed. He experienced the horrible fear that Liz was going to pull over to the curb and tell him to get out. Dump him. Yes, there was a reason she was thinking about the word dump. He waited for her to stop the car and say, 'Just get out.'

But she did not.

Catching her breath, the woman who represented a financially secure future, pressed on the gas pedal again and said two words he hated for Liz to say, "Never mind."

And then they drove in silence the next three miles to the church. It was a narrow street with old houses, and most of them had some kind of decoration. The efforts were often humble and straggly. But there was something very encouraging about even the most humble bits of tinsel and color festively tied to a front door or sometimes a big red ribbon secured to the mailbox. The small efforts displayed a great effort at hospitality—of cheering the community at large during the holiday season.

The City of Montgomery always put up a big Christmas tree downtown, but Mark could not see it from his house. He had not taken the time to go look at it. When he thought about the

City's Christmas tree, he realized that he lived very close to it, but he had only ever seen the community Christmas tree on television on the six o'clock news when they showed the dramatic first lighting of it. People clapped.

"You would not know what I am trying to say. It is okay. We are just different people."

Turning toward her, he said, "You do look lovely tonight."

Liz brightened instantly. She checked her appearance in the rear-view mirror, adopting an expression that people who take selfies often wear. Mouth pursed. Eyebrows raised. Chin lowered.

"I try," Liz said with a heavy sigh. "That is all I can do. Try."

The car slowed as they reached the back entrance to the parking lot and cars were making their way in, but not without stopping first.

"What in heaven's name is that?" Liz breathed the question.

The car slowed again, this time to a crawl.

"What is what?" Mark asked, leaning forward to peer at what she was seeing. An older lady dressed as an elf was pointing this way and that to drivers when they entered. "Is someone collecting a parking fee in a church parking lot? Someone dressed like an elf?" he asked.

The idea triggered stark terror. He would have to feign a search in his pockets for a five-dollar bill, and he did not have a five-dollar bill on him. It was eight days to the first of the next month—next year! -- and his social security check did not get deposited right away.

Sometimes the money appeared in his bank account around the 5th day of the month. He had been wondering about what he could sell to get a little cash to tide him over. He touched his cufflinks. They were not worth anything. Not really.

"An elf?" Liz asked, squinting.

Cars intending to turn into the parking lot slowed as they came to the threshold entrance to the church parking lot and tried to discern the purpose of the older woman wearing green shorts with black tights, a white blouse, and a pair of brown reindeer ears. When they reached where the elf was standing, she motioned for them to keep going left.

What a relief.

The elf was only directing traffic--not collecting for some kind of children's orphanage or the Community Food Bank. Mark no longer answered his front door when people came knocking on it and asking for money for different charitable needs like the Community Food Bank.

It occurred to him in that moment that if he could find out where the Food Bank was located he could go. He was what they called Food Insecure. He could go to a food bank and get some food. He could do that. Maybe it was within walking distance because his station wagon was less than half full of gas; and if he could walk, he could save the rest of the gas for later. Later. Later. It seemed to Mark Gardiner like his whole life was suspended while he waited on later to materialize and be better than the present moment of his life.

8

A BLEAK MIDWINTER

"That is the craziest thing I have ever seen here," Liz mumbled.

The parking lot elf hopped back and forth from one foot to the other as she gesticulated to incoming drivers which way to steer. Her movements were elaborate, the signals with both hands insistent: *You go that way and park over there. You? You go the other way.*

"Don't you have a regular place where you park?" Mark asked Liz, trying to sit taller. Discomfort, hunger, tooth pain, and a kind of fatalism that he was not going to be able to save himself this time was beating him down. He felt himself slumping from time to time, and he was trying not to give way to that. Old men slumped. Younger men stood tall. Sat tall.

'Don't let the old man in.'

That is what Clint Eastwood said, and he was older than Mark. "Don't let the old man in," Mark whispered to himself.

"I am going to park here tonight," Liz said with finality. "Today," she amended. It was just three-twenty in the afternoon.

"There goes poor Mildred Budge," she stated, as they watched Jake driving that old Mercedes find the perfect parking spot right near the best door to use. Mildred and Chase got out of the car and walked around to Jake who was waiting for them both.

"Poor Mildred Budge," Liz repeated, shaking her head. "Riding around in that deathtrap of a car. Poor Mildred Budge."

"What do you mean, poor?" Mark asked. He did not move to open his door. Liz did not eject herself from the car before checking her lipstick in the mirror again. He knew to wait for that or she would be impatient with him for coming around to get her prematurely.

"Oh, look at what she is wearing. This is not Halloween. She has got on some kind of witchy skirt, though I do not think a witch would wear that while riding on her best broomstick."

Liz laughed at her own description. "Well, at least it is not brown. Mildred Budge loves brown. But she is wearing that awful old-timey skirt and going into church dragging that orphan boy, who is a dim bulb by any standard, and that, that…. well, that black man she is keeping company with. He has never been married."

"How do you know that?" Mark interrupted. His hand reached for the car door and he pressed on it, feeling it give way. He pushed it open slightly. It was cold outside, but he needed some air.

"Because I would know if he had been married," Liz replied curtly. "If it is one thing I know it is who is married and who is not," she declared.

Liz resumed her commentary, changing her tone to one of condolence rather than criticism. There was only a slight difference, but there was one. That difference caused Mark to let go of the car door. 'Let her say it,' he thought. 'She will either say it now or later.'

"Poor Mildred. She never had a chance in life really. For the best part of her life when she could have been out living life and having fun, she taught hundreds of smelly little kids in school rooms that didn't have air conditioning. She took care of both parents until they finally died and became a blessed memory."

"I have heard that expression before," Mark said.

"What?" Liz demanded, irritated that her speech had been interrupted.

"When people die they become a blessed memory. As if memory is always in the past." He did not say more, and Liz did not ask, who is your blessed memory?

She did not want to know.

"Would you just let me finish what I am trying to say?" she asked, exasperated.

Mark lapsed into the kind of enduring silence that he had known before with other women like her. They wore you down--women like Liz--and there were a lot of them.

"What I am trying to say," she began slowly. "Is that Mildred Budge didn't have much of a life, and so she doesn't know now that she doesn't have much of a life."

When Mark did not interrupt her again, Liz began to explain Mildred Budge with more confidence. "She is raising some other woman's kid, and he is a special-needs child, which is just the truth, not anything more than that. And she is dating a black man who has never been married. Bless her heart. She doesn't know about men."

Liz waited to see if Mark would interrupt her again.

"Women of her generation were not raised to date black men. I wonder what her parents would think."

"I think people forget his color. And hers," Mark said, defending two people in that moment that he would like to be his friends. It surged up in him—a feeling that he didn't let himself have often. He would like for Jake and Mildred to be his friends. Yes, he would like for both of them to be his friends.

"We can talk about this some other time," Liz said, irritably. "Or not. People do not have to think the same way. I forget that you used to live in California and...." Her brow furrowed. Her manicured hands plucked at a rhinestone buckle she had pinned to her black velvet clutch handbag in her lap. She said with resignation, "You are a liberal, aren't you?"

Mark thought about saying, no. He thought about trying to tell Liz that words which lumped people into ill-defined categories made him feel heavy and worn down. Beat down. He was already so beat down that he didn't have the strength to use one more word that dehumanized people.

Instead, Mark simply said, "I believe I am. Yes, I believe I must be a liberal, because I forget Jake is black, and I do not think Mildred being white and raising an abandoned boy means she is poor Mildred Budge. I think she is just Mildred Budge, and he is just Jake Diamond, and something about who each one of them is seems to be just what the other person needs."

Liz grew deadly still.

"I did not know you still thought about her."

Mark didn't reply. The silence punished them both.

"There is a lot about you I do not know," she said coldly.

"That is right," Mark agreed, his mouth going dry from the strain of the conversation. He was parched. *Was there a water fountain inside? And if he could get a cold sip of it would the water hurt that bad tooth in the back?* "There is a lot about me you don't know," he agreed.

Liz changed instantly. Instantly. He thought she would lower the visor with the little light and check her make-up again. But she did not.

Instead, his date for Christmas Eve fixed a forced smile on her face that almost scared him and said words that sounded like a threat: "The night is young. In fact, it is still afternoon. Who knows what kind of Christmas we are going to have?"

9

ON BORROWED TIME

Holding her purse tightly, Liz waited for Mark to come around the car and open the door for her.

"What do you think of these shoes?" Liz asked pertly as she swung her legs out of the car and planted them on the asphalt of the church parking lot.

Mark caught himself. He almost said, 'Aren't they the same ones you always wear?' But they were not, or she would not have asked.

"Classy," Mark replied. *Classy was a safe answer.*

Liz smoothed the back of her dress, tugging at the sides to make it reach her knees, almost, caressed her diamond choker necklace, fingered the pearls on her pearl necklace, and then checked both ear lobes to make sure she had not lost a diamond earring.

Mark watched, feeling inadequate to be wearing his old best clothes and a small diamond tie clasp he had won in a golf tournament twenty-five years ago. He had pawned it twice and gotten it back both times.

She took his arm without his offering it, and Mark inhaled deeply, scanning the sky, and stifling a chill. He had not worn an overcoat.

"Looks like rain," he observed.

"Someone said it might snow," Liz replied.

"Snow," he repeated with a repressed shiver.

His house was cold. He did not use much heat because he could not afford to pay a big power bill. On days when the weather was dark and icy, he stayed inside the mausoleum called his house looking over the Alabama River because he did not have an overcoat. He had a fireplace though, and he used that when he had some wood. Fortunately, after a storm that felled a tree, people often put wood out on the street for the city to pick up. Whenever Mark saw some wood on the curb, he stopped and piled it in the back of his station wagon. He had a good stack of wood now in the back of his house, and remembering that comforted him. Maybe he would build a fire tonight after Liz left. Yes, maybe he would have a fire for Christmas.

Liz stopped walking suddenly.

"What is it?" Mark asked. He stifled a shiver, hoping she would not notice how cold he was.

"Did you see that?" Liz asked. Her eyes were wide, her mouth open, and she pointed upward toward the roof of the church and the top of a tall white column that was more likely for show than support of the roof.

"I don't see anything," Mark said, as the church door opened.

Light spilled out from the church onto the concrete entranceway, as Jake held the door open for Mildred and Chase.

Jake Diamond was every man's competition: strong, athletic, well- dressed in good quality clothes, and he wore a healthy smile.

"There," Liz said quietly. "There. Up there! I do not mean that man. Jake. Do you see what I see up there on the column? There." Liz said the word again.

She did not tell her new boyfriend that she had a history of seeing angels of death flying over the heads of men; and when she saw one, a man she knew always died soon after. She looked wistfully at Jake, who was now holding the door open for Sam and Belle.

"Wait. Let's not rush the old folks," Liz said. Maybe the angel of death was for Sam. He was on his way to heaven anyway. That is not what people said, but that was the truth.

"Let the old folks get inside. Then, we will go inside."

And just as soon as Liz announced the plan something zoomed past Belle's head, past Sam's ear, past Jake holding open the door, and into the church building.

"I saw that," Mark said. "I saw a bird. I think it was a pigeon. I think a pigeon flew into the church building."

Relief flooded Liz Luckie. "It was just a bird? You are sure?"

"Sure, I am sure," Mark replied, though just that quickly he was not sure. It had to be a bird, didn't it? "It could have been a bat, I suppose, but I do not think bats fly into the light. They fly away from it."

"As long as it is not...." Liz said.

Mark waited, but she was gripping his arm tightly now, as Jake had followed Belle and Sam into the church, letting the door fall softly behind them. Now Mark was going to have to yank the heavy church door back open, and he would have to make opening the heavy door look effortless. Mark flexed his hand in and out, warming it up. His hand was tingling. It did that now. Was that tingling from time-to-time a symptom of some disease, like Parkinson's? Sometimes, the aged former movie actor felt as if he were living on borrowed time. He had been healthy for so long, surely the other dreaded shoe would drop, and he would pay a dear price for having worked outdoors in the sunshine for as long as he had.

"Come on, Lady Luck. Let me get you inside that warm building and out of this cold," he prompted, leading the way.

Liz flinched at the nickname. She had buried four husbands she had loved desperately. How could anyone call her lucky? Mark had very long legs, and she had very short legs. She no longer felt like walking double-time to keep up with anyone. At this stage in her life, Liz was no longer ready to hurry and match her stride to any man's.

Mark strode ahead to reach the door first and yanked the heavy door back. Warm air rushed toward him. He leaned into it, waiting for Liz to enter. Then he followed her.

Stepping into the warm foyer, Mark smiled. The tall Christmas tree was lit up, brilliant, colorful, and decorated beautifully.

Liz gasped. "Who would have thought that a Podunk town like this one would have a tree that chic?"

Liz had no sooner asked the question when an ornament fell and hit the top of one of her buckled shoes. A cluster of rhinestones popped off and scattered. Liz looked up and saw the pigeon trying to hide in the top branches. An angel ornament on top trembled mightily.

"Gracious!" Liz remarked, wondering if she was supposed to laugh.

"I told you it was a bird, darling."

Liz smiled. "Yes. I like that," she approved. "I like darling."

"Darling," Mark repeated.

And she smiled as they heard Jake Diamond tell Mildred Budge and Chase to go find a good seat and get comfortable and that he would catch up with them. As Director of Outreach and Chairman of Missions, he needed to touch base with Kathryn Harris, who was overseeing the baking of the sugar cookies in the church kitchen.

10

DIAMOND JAKE

As Liz and Mark approached the church kitchen on their way to the sanctuary, they heard ladies laughing on the other side of the swinging door.

Laughing. In church.

Water was running in the sink.

Pans were banging.

Timers beeped. Cookies crisped.

"I will get them out this time," a church lady offered.

"We need another platter so this batch can cool," another volunteer replied.

"God forbid, we serve warm cookies!"

More laughter.

"What are we going to do with all of the broken cookies?"

"They will eat just as good."

And then the door to the kitchen closed, and Mark could not hear any more.

***

"I am stopping at the ladies' room first. Wait for me," Liz commanded.

Mark's empty stomach clenched. He nodded that he would wait. His jaw ached. Wasn't that a symptom of a heart attack, too? Maybe he didn't have a bad tooth. Maybe he had a bad heart. The idea scared him. His jaw throbbed.

Uncomfortable and wishing he could sit down, Mark studied the closed door to the kitchen. Life was happening on the other side. The smell of freshly baked cookies was tantalizing. It had been a while since anyone had offered him a cookie warm from the oven. Or even a cold broken one.

And just as that regret surfaced, causing him to feel older than his years, Mark heard a woman with a friendly voice urge, "Oh, Jake. Have another cookie on the house."

So Jake Diamond was on the other side of that closed door inside with the ladies where all the action was and the kind of place Mark Gardiner used to be: in the heart of it all, not on the outside eavesdropping while he waited uncomfortably for a woman to fix her face one more time. Liz and her face!

Hunger gnawed at him. His stomach growled.

Mark peered hard at the closed kitchen door. What would happen if he just pushed open that door and asked in his friendliest radio voice, "What is going on? Got room for one more?"

For an instant Mark thought, if I could go through that door and it closed, Liz would not be able to find me when she returned. The relief in his shoulders was immediate and immense. He could take a deeper breath. Even that aching tooth in the back seemed to lessen its throbbing. Mark wondered distractedly in that moment if he really had a toothache. Maybe Liz Luckie was the cause of his jaw ache. Maybe it was tension in his jaw, and she was the cause of that tension. Maybe he could just walk away from her. Maybe he could just walk through that door; and when Liz returned, she wouldn't know where he was. The idea brought him no comfort, because Liz was Plan A, and he did not have a Plan B.

Once upon a time, Mark would have been in there making good-natured ladies laugh and eating their cookies. Instantly, he experienced a pang that did not have a name, but he felt a kind of yearning for yesterday and who he once had been. And it was that feeling of yearning for who he had been that caused him not to hear Liz reappear.

Liz's voice broke into his reverie. "If that is what you think you like, you have got the wrong girl. I am not one of them—one of those ladies who bakes cookies," Liz sniffed. "And I never will be, so if that is what you want, you are going to be disappointed."

It took a couple of seconds for Liz's voice to reach Mark. Her warning echoed for a while as he thought about the past and wondered what he was going to do about getting some food into his refrigerator at home and how much longer did he need to spend with Liz before he gave up? He had not really confronted that question: when should he give up on Liz and set a different goal?

Maybe he could sell his big old house and clear enough to move and start over somewhere else. Could he make a move like that?

If he wanted to sell the house, it needed to be upgraded. It needed repairs, and he did not have the money to pay for them.

He was stuck--trapped by being older and not having money. He would need a financial windfall to start over, and he did not have a bonanza opportunity in his sights.

Mark was beat down and could not envision other options, and he had gone through the ones he knew about.

Liz tugged on his sleeve. "Really?" she asked. "Are you just going to stand there daydreaming on Memory Lane, or are we going to find a seat and get through this Christmas Eve service?"

Mark tried to stand taller. That move often helped him get through an evening with Liz.

The ladies in the kitchen were still laughing and bustling. Mark knew he needed to move, but he could not make himself leave the sounds of happiness on the other side of that kitchen door.

He listened to those sounds hungrily, thirstily, enviously.

"Oh, Jake, you are a diamond in the rough. That is what you are. We are going to put you a bunch of these broken cookies together in a bag so you can take them home and eat the ones we cannot serve."

"I am happy with the crumbs from your tables, ladies," Jake assured them. It was a gallant response—the kind that Mark used to say when he was the center of attention among a group of playful ladies.

Mark knew what the cookies would be in Jake's to-go bag. There would be only a few broken ones, and a dozen oversized ones: the best from the cookie sheets, and the ladies would all know he would enjoy them later. They wanted him to do just that.

The good women used to dote on Mark Gardiner. The woman beside him did not have a doting bone in her body.

The swinging door opened fully once more as a bemused church lady came out bearing a tray of sugar cookies. Kathryn's face lit up when she saw Mark and Liz.

"Hello, you two beautiful people!" she said. "Glad you could make it! The early bird gets the sugar cookies," she said, holding out the platter for Liz and Mark to take a warm cookie.

Instantly, Mark's pang of homesickness for who he used to be eased.

The woman in front of him had a bright smile, and it stayed on her face.

Mark smiled back, honestly. Something in him that had grown dormant began to wake up. A real smile from someone else can bring out a real smile in anyone.

"You are here early," Kathryn Harris said, acknowledging Liz with the same smile, though it changed slightly.

"We do want a good seat," Liz explained.

"Are you staying for cookies and hot apple cider?" Kathryn asked, without waiting for an answer. "Because we are going to have a great time. Christmas Eve is the best night of the year," Kathryn promised. "Liz, are you eating cookies tonight? Want one now?" she asked, still holding out the platter.

Mark reached out and took a cookie. He took a bite while Liz was still thinking about it.

"They are still warm. Cinnamon. Sugar. And, do not tell anybody, but we even shaved a bit of fresh ginger into some of the cookies just because...."

"Because you ladies are not afraid to live," Mark interjected quickly. He popped the rest of the cookie in his mouth and chewed. It was the best thing he had eaten in weeks.

He wondered if the lady with the tray of warm cookies was married. There were several well-off widows in the church, and she was friendly enough not to be married. You can tell things like that about a lady if you know how to read women. Yes. Yes. The woman in front of him could very easily become Plan B. He began to take heart.

Liz shook her head. "I don't eat cookies this time of day," she said.

Liz had just reapplied her lipstick in the ladies' room, and she did not want to mess it up. Further, she did not want crumbs from a cookie sticking to her fur-trimmed jacket or bespeckling her black velvet dress.

"Monty, want a cookie?

"Who?" Mark asked.

"Your name is not Monty?" the church lady asked, tipping the tray of sugar cookies in his direction again. He took another cookie.

"Don't mind if I do," he said. "I have a motto. When temptation like this knocks, I answer the door."

Liz eyed him suspiciously. "His name isn't Monty. It's Mark," Liz replied coldly. And then looking at Mark she asked scornfully, "Why would you say something like that about temptation in church?"

Kathryn laughed, and said, "I have already eaten three. I think they are good this year. We are playing around with the recipe."

For an instant, Mark thought that Liz might be two-timing him with some guy named Monty and everyone knew it but him, and then Mark realized he was just being paranoid. The smiling lady just could not remember his name.

"I am Mark. I am with her," he said, tipping his head toward Liz.

Liz's grip on his bent left arm tightened in the presence of the other woman.

That tightened grip did not mean Liz wanted Mark more. It meant she did not want anyone else to have him.

"I am Kathryn Harris," the cookie bearer said.

He marveled at her smile. She could smile at will and would be envied by everyone who could not. He wished he could smile like that.

"Apologies! Of course your name is Mark. It is coming back to me. You are a Master Gardener. That is right. Your name is Mark Gardiner, and you used to be on the radio. You have got a radio voice! That is right. Am I right?"

He nodded. "I have been on the radio." He did not add that he had once had some bit parts in movies, too. A long time ago he used to brag about that, but his acting career had never taken off. Now, if he mentioned his very small parts from so long ago in forgettable old movies, he would simply sound like a has been—or a never was.

"I am good with names, but not as good as I once was," Kathryn explained. "I do not know why I thought your name was Monty, but it came to me just now. Monty Hall. That is the name of the man who used to host that game show, *Let's Make a Deal.*

You kind of look like him too." Her gaze swept up. "How tall are you?" she asked bluntly.

"Tall enough," he said with a grin that he had copied from an old-timey actor who had made his fortune off a lazy smile.

"Liz, you will never lose him because you can see him anywhere."

Liz's eyes grew dark, and she held tightly onto Mark. "I don't intend to lose him," she said, and her voice was steely.

It was the nicest thing Liz Luckie had ever said about Mark to other people, and now Mark smiled, stepping an inch closer to Liz, grateful to the smiling woman in front of him who had caused his date to make such a claim. It was progress. Yes, it was certainly progress.

"Oh, Monty Hall was a handsome thing. But then, you have heard that before," she teased. She was not flirting exactly. He had learned over time that women in the South often used what sounded like flirting in everyday conversation, but for them, it was just being polite.

"Don't let us keep you," Liz said, tugging at Mark. "We better go get our seat. I hear people coming in behind us."

The door to the kitchen swung open again. There were half a dozen women in there laughing and moving around with spatulas and cookie sheets. One woman stood at the sink washing a big bowl.

This time it was Jake acting like he was going to come out but not exiting entirely. They were teasing him.

"Oh, don't fret yourself, Diamond Jake. We have enough cookies this year. And this place over here next to the microwave—this is where your personal bag of broken cookies will be. Do not forget it. You will not starve to death with us looking after you."

A bag of broken cookie pieces sounded like heaven on earth to Mark Gardiner.

Mark mentally planned Jake's response as he said the words: "I am counting on you ladies to keep me from going hungry."

It was a good line.

Kathryn smiled toward the kitchen and the ladies talking with Jake.

"That's Jake Diamond, but some of us call him Diamond Jake because...well, just because he is a keeper," Kathryn Harris explained. "You two love birds better hurry on into the sanctuary now so you can get a good seat."

"Catch you later," Mark said quietly, as Kathryn walked off holding the tray of cookies.

She was taking them to the reception room.

"We will get a cookie afterwards if you are so hungry," Liz said. "What was the point in coming early if we do not go find a seat?"

"I am all yours," Mark promised, as Liz nudged him toward the sanctuary.

***

An usher was holding open the door.

"No program tonight," he announced.

"Good," Liz replied. She did not like to have to keep up with a program in church. Then, she stopped briefly in the doorway to tidy herself with little pats here and there to arrange her features. Liz even had a half-smile that she wore from time-to-time.

Her entrance was ruined by the pigeon, which flew over their heads toward the back of the sanctuary where the people sat who did not care if they got a cookie or not sat on Christmas Eve.

Liz yelped.

Mark patted his hair. The pigeon had brushed his head flying by.

Then Liz asked the strangest question in a little girl voice Mark had never heard her use before. "That was a bird, wasn't it?"

11

MUSIC ON CHRISTMAS EVE

"Jake, is it like this every year?" Steev asked. The whole day had been miserable. He had fielded irate phone calls from church-goers still upset about the one Christmas Eve service. Others were calling in to say that they couldn't do the jobs they had agreed to do. Steev was overwhelmed by the number of problems that he wasn't sure could be solved by four o'clock.

"Where's the program?" Jake asked, distractedly.

Steev shook his. "We had a problem with it. We don't have one," he said. He didn't explain that Janie had produced a program, but there were so many errors in it that he had thrown the whole two hundred copies in the trashcan. There hadn't been time to fix the mistakes and reprint the program.

"And now, we have lost our piano player and the narrator for the nativity skit," Steev said. "I don't think you can do both jobs."

"Nope," Jake said, and he felt his own smile fade. He wanted to sit with Mildred and Chase and savor Christmas Eve with them. It would have been the first time in a very long time when he would have felt as if he were with his own family during the service. He wanted to know that—to live it. Instead, he was going to have to work on Christmas Eve.

"We need you to play the old carols while the kids come out and perform the nativity. And, we need someone to read the Bethlehem script who is not afraid to read a script in front of people. If I must, I can read the script; but then people will be tired of listening to me, and I still must give a homily," Steev said, as he spied Kathryn Harris over by the left side door that led to the prayer room.

She had the children in there who were playing parts in the nativity scene. She still had Mary, Joseph, and three wise men, but she was down to one angel. Steev had heard a dog bark earlier and did not have the energy to ask why he could hear a dog in the building.

Steev needed to tell Miss Kathryn that they had lost the narrator, but usually when he reported a problem he had an idea of what to do to solve it. It was his first Christmas Eve as the new preacher of the Church on the Corner, and he had more problems than solutions.

Kathryn Harris sensed a tension between the two men and crossed the room to find out what it was. "What has happened now?"

Steev replied succinctly. "Buster has laryngitis."

"Laryngitis?" she repeated, dubious. She had known Buster a long time. He was not the sickly type. But he was a six o'clocker. The four o'clock service was a sore point with him, and she guessed he was making a point by calling in sick.

Steev nodded seriously. "He told me so himself in a voice that was a bit stronger than you expect to hear when someone cannot talk."

Kathryn nodded. "I have heard rumblings. Aren't people funny," she mused.

"You can call it that," Steev said. "We also lost our piano player. Jake is going to fill in."

"Good for you, Jake," Kathryn said, growing still and concentrated. She could feel her blood pressure rising. If she had to, she supposed she could read that script. But she also needed to direct the children to go in and come out. Who would do that if she read the script? The script was simple. All you had to do was read it. Anyone could read it. And then she saw Mark squeezed in uncomfortably beside Liz on the sixth pew, his left leg stretching out into the aisle. He dragged it back in quickly when someone needed to pass by.

She pointed discreetly toward Mark. "He used to be on the radio."

"I have heard that," Steev admitted. "I just don't know the man very well."

"Mark is an old friend of mine," she said. "Give me a second," Kathryn asked, walking off before anyone could object.

Mark sensed Kathryn coming toward them before she reached him, and that part of him that had stood on the other side of the kitchen door and eavesdropped on the ladies came back to life again. The pretty lady with the honest smile was searching his face. That was a good sign. The smiling lady was not coming to see Liz.

"Mark, we need your help," Kathryn announced immediately, leaning forward. The intensity of the announcement dismissed the expectation of small talk.

Mark stood up; the way men did when greeting a lady. "I saw the pigeon, too," he confirmed. "I am tall, but I am not that tall," he said with his best lazy grin.

"Mark is not here to catch your pigeon," Liz objected.

Kathryn nodded and smiled. "It is not about the pigeon. Our narrator for the children's nativity skit has laryngitis, and we were wondering if you would be comfortable using your radio voice to read the script for us. It is not very long." She hesitated. "It only runs about ten minutes."

It had been years since anyone had asked Mark to use his radio voice. Years.

He blinked rapidly, the first sign of a stage fright that he had forgotten ever existed in him. He swallowed hard, wondering with a dawning anxiety if he could do it. Could he read a simple script for a children's nativity scene?

"How big is the type on the page?" Mark asked suddenly, growing serious. He had other questions, but that was the important one. The problem was that he did not have his reading glasses with him. Liz did not even know he used reading glasses.

Kathryn grinned broadly, deepening the crow's feet around her eyes. She knew the wrinkles were there and deepening with each laugh, but she did not care. The church lady loved smiling more than she feared the prospect of wrinkles. "I know the answer to that question. It is 14 point, bold-faced."

Mark nodded, as if they were both suddenly speaking a foreign language the two of them understood, but Liz did not.

Liz frowned. "Mark is off-duty tonight. It is Christmas Eve."

She was acting like his agent, and that was almost the final straw.

Mark Gardiner, the actor, chose his own agents, and if he were choosing one, it would not be Liz Luckie.

"The show must go on," Mark said, stepping out into the aisle. "Where do you want me to be?"

"With me for a while. When it is time, you will go up the steps over there to the side of the pulpit and read from that black music stand. When you go out to the music stand, a spotlight will come on. You will be able to see the words on the page," she promised him.

"The show must go on," Mark repeated, and despite his toothache, he grinned.

"I will give Mark back when this is over, Lizzie," Kathryn promised as he stepped out into the aisle and fell into step behind her.

"In the meantime, let's get you some warm apple cider. It is good for the voice. And maybe a kitchen sandwich. We volunteers have been snacking on them all afternoon. You will need your blood sugar stabilized. If you are like me, you have been too busy to eat. The holidays are hard," Kathryn said, leading the way to the anteroom below the pulpit steps where the children's nativity script was stored in a folder.

It was a drafty room near the missions' clothes closet; and once she was there, Kathryn felt a chill. "This is the coldest spot in the whole building. Look in that missions closet there and find yourself some kind of coat to wear."

Just that quickly, she stopped him. "Wait a minute. Let me do that," she said. "I think I remember a coat that will fit you."

Mark said nothing, just stood by while another woman took charge of his wardrobe. He heard Kathryn pushing hangers, talking as much to herself as to him. "Too short. Too small. Too....old."

Mark heard Kathryn rip a garment off its hanger and saw a jacket drop to the floor, her head shaking. "These donated clothes are supposed to be gently used. That one had been worn to death. Wait a minute; here it is—the coat I was thinking of."

Mark saw Kathryn remove a long black wool coat from its hanger which had been pushed way in the back.

"I remember this coat. It belonged to Hugh. Hang on. That might create a problem with Liz. If I am right, this coat belonged to Liz's last husband."

'Last husband?' Mark wanted to ask, 'How many has she had?,' but he stopped himself just in time. Instead, he said, "I didn't know him."

Kathryn held the practically new black wool coat out in front of her. "It looks like a hundred other coats. Liz may not even make the connection. They were not married very long," she mused. "It is so cold back here. If you can wear this, do. It will keep you from shivering while you are trying to read the words."

Mark shrugged his arms into the long wool coat, feeling the weight of the wool and the potential warmth that would come soon enough. He felt strange in that moment, wondering if he had looked like he needed a coat or if this smiling woman was truly responding to the penetrating chill in the anteroom. In the shadows, Mark did not need to guard the expression on his face. In the shadows with a kind woman tending to him, he just let her.

"This place is so draughty," she said. "It is a wonder we do not all catch a chill. Is that okay?"

He felt his fingertips grip the cuffs of the coat sleeves. "It will do," he said, sounding as if he were doing her a favor by wearing the costume she had picked out for him.

"We are going to have to winnow out that closet. It is too full. If you can use that coat, keep it. We need to thin out that closet," she repeated, thinking ahead to the new year when she and a friend would come over and pare down the missions closet. "I have got to go check on the kids. The script is right there, if you want to read it through a couple of times."

Mark nodded and flipped open the script. It was a large font, and it was printed in bold. He could see the words. "I am on it," he assured her.

"I will be standing on the other side right there," Kathryn said, pointing. "When you hear Jake play *O Little Town of Bethlehem* that is your cue. Go up those three steps and then over to the black music stand. Until then, there is a chair. Let yourself get comfortable. Someone from the kitchen will bring you a snack and a cup of warm cider. I think that will help you," she said. "Anything else?"

"A Tylenol?" he asked. That back tooth was throbbing.

"Coming right up," she said. "We keep them in the kitchen next to the Band-aids and the Tums. I think I will take one, too.

Thanks for the reminder," she said. "Just hang tight. It is all coming together."

Mark reviewed his instructions after Kathryn left him in the anteroom. There was a small set of steps that led upward to the stage and the pulpit where the preacher would stand. There was a piano. An organ. A microphone in front of that black music stand where he would be positioned. On the stage. In a spotlight. And there was the pigeon sitting on one of the organ's silver pipes.

"Oh, you darling you," a woman said, as she bustled in with a small plate of finger sandwiches and a cup of steaming apple cider. "You have really saved the day. Thank you for jumping into the breach. We needed you so much. Kathryn told me to bring you these."

Mark stared at the saucer with four chicken salad finger sandwiches on it. He had never seen anything that looked as appetizing as those little sandwiches. "I did not bring you a cookie, but you can have one. I did not think of it. I could get you one?" she offered.

"Just a Tylenol, if that wouldn't be too much trouble," he asked.

"That is right. Kathryn said to bring you a Tylenol," she remembered. "I have them here." She reached into her pocket and produced a small red and white bottle. She popped the lid off, her hands shaking. "Don't mind me. I shake, but I am not scared. It is just a tremble—the kind that just happens to you," she said, holding the Tylenol bottle over Mark's open palm.

His hand trembled slightly, too, from being cold and hungry. At first, he was embarrassed, and then he was not. The church lady paid no attention to the anxiety displayed in his trembling hand. Instead, she shook out what was supposed to be two pills, but a half dozen tablets fell out.

"Take what you want now, and put the rest in your pocket for later. We cannot put them back in the bottle once they have fallen out."

Mark nodded, keeping two white tablets and the other four pills in his left coat pocket. They were gold to him. He would have them for later. Maybe they would help him with the tooth pain, and he could sleep through the night.

"Thank you," he said, reaching for the apple cider. He took a warm sip. It tasted very good. He put the two tablets in his mouth and swallowed them with the next sip.

"There are water bottles in that cabinet," she said. "Sometimes cider makes me thirsty."

He opened the cabinet and saw a dozen bottles of water. "Got it," he said. "And what is your name?"

"I am Moe. Maureen, really. But people call me Moe. I like it."

"Moe," he repeated. "I am Mark." And when he introduced himself to her and repeated her name he felt a burden lift, for there was nothing in the moment that made him feel as if he had to create Plan C or Plan D. He just needed to let his Tylenol work, eat his four chicken salad finger sandwiches, drink that hot apple cider, and read through that script.

"I have got to scoot, Mark. But there is a men's room right through there if you want to wash up. It is not bigger than a closet, but the boys who work here use it. You are going to be great. Thank you so much for stepping up when we needed you most."

"A great pleasure," he replied gallantly.

Moe beamed. It was a Christmas Eve moment that warmed Mark more than the coat from the missions closet that he might sleep in for the rest of the winter nights.

1 2

ALL HANDS ON
DECK THE HALLS

"Jake, if you want to go out and start playing some music while people are settling in, that would be good," Steev encouraged. Agreeing with himself, Steev added, "Yes, that would be good. And when people are leaving to go to the reception room, if you could play some more then, that would be good."

Jake saw Steev remember that there was a small spinet piano in the reception room. He saw his friend consider asking Jake to pick up playing more Christmas carols there too, but then Steev caught a look on Jake's face and kept the idea to himself.

'Good,' Jake thought. 'My Christmas spirit only goes so far.'

"Now?" Jake asked, his gaze sweeping the congregation. The pews on the ground floor were packed. Looking up, he saw the balcony was full, too.

"Now," Steev agreed. "I hope you didn't have something else you needed to do."

Jake did not want to tell Steev the truth. He wanted to sit with Mildred and Chase and enjoy the evening. But he didn't say the words that would have added to Steev's tension. Instead, Jake said, "Will I see you at Mildred's later?"

"Oh, sure. Though it is going to be an early night for me. I have got another sermon to write for Sunday."

"They roll around," Jake replied automatically.

"Okay. You are set. The children in the skit are waiting in the prayer room, and Kathryn Harris will send them in on time. She has got Liz's boyfriend standing by in my anteroom over there to do the narration. When you start playing *O Little Town of Bethlehem* that is the cue for the skit. She will lead them out then, and the boyfriend....."

"Mark," Jake reminded him. "It is Mark something."

Steev nodded silently, checking off items on his mental to-do list.

And that is when it began to hit Steev hard. It was his first big Christmas at the Church on the Corner, and while people had been liking the new preacher's Sunday sermons—not everybody but a lot of people seemed to—they wanted a good Christmas event to start the next year. His honeymoon period at the Church on the Corner was over, and reality was beginning.

"Let me tell Millie what's going on, and then I will go to the piano," Jake said.

Steev nodded, but he was distracted. They had about fifteen minutes if they started on time. What would happen if they started late?

He was off his game. He was simply off his game. Steev knew that was not exactly the truth, but it was the easiest way to explain to himself that he was not ready to preach a Christmas Eve sermon. Not even a homily.

He was not at peace with himself, and all the ways that he knew to get back into the zone that suited him best were not working.

Steev was exercising every day, going for early morning runs through the neighborhood before most people turned on their kitchen lights and flipped the coffee pot switch. Exercise was not enough. He was not himself. Not his best self, anyway. And he could not seem to fix it.

And he knew why. He could not stop thinking about Janie. Maybe giving her the job as the receptionist here at the church had been a terrible mistake. Good for her with that baby. Bad for him because he could not stop thinking about her.

The problem was he did not want to think about Janie. He was not ready to settle down. What he really wanted to do was work on a doctorate. He could do much of the classwork online and then grab a few days during the week here and there to go to Atlanta for in-person classes. He could do that and hold down this job.

The best solution to his Janie problem that he could come up with was to not be alone with her. But every single day he resolved to keep a professional distance, they ended up together and alone, and he was aware of her in the way that he did not want to be aware of her. Whenever he had to go and see her in that little desk space where she answered the phone, he purposed to make it short. *Do business. Leave.* But then, the phone would ring. Baby Sam would cry because the phone had rung; and while Janie was comforting him, Steev would answer the phone call. By the time he got off the phone Janie would be standing beside him very close, and he could feel her breathing and know the fragrance of her shampoo and the lingering sweetness of the baby, and he began to think: 'She is not temptation. She is the answer to a prayer I have been afraid to make because I do need a wife and a family, and she and the baby are right here. Maybe I need a family more than another degree.'

When Steev considered that, he wondered what it would be like to have them living in his house and would he have enough space to write his sermons and study and pray? A lot of people in the world did not understand how much quiet time you needed to stay prepped to preach. Mildred Budge knew. They had talked about it. Jake understood to a certain extent. But even his own mother had not known the cost on his private life to stay ready to preach in what was called in one way 'practicing the Presence.' It was a day-to-day lifelong discipline.

Just thinking about Janie stopped Steev in his tracks. Once Steev started, he could not stop. His preaching mind took a back seat to the remembered sound of Janie breathing and the sudden light in her pale grey eyes when she saw him approach. He was fascinated by the movement of her hand across the desktop, trailing its surface when she reached for a pen to write a message and how she brushed her reddish-brown hair out of her eyes and the shy confession that, yes, she did have a small tattoo of a dragonfly in a place no one could see. And he had wanted to see the dragonfly tattoo, and in the wanting, the young preacher was off his game.

And it was Christmas Eve.

There was no stand-in for the preacher.

No one to fill in as Kathryn had for three other women, as Jake was doing for the piano player, and now as Mark was doing for Buster.

Steev wanted to preach, but he just was not ready.

He had a short message, but it was not a homily. It was the outline for an essay he had written to apply for the doctoral program. He had deconstructed the key symbols of the Christmas story, showing how culture had misinterpreted the events and turned the story of the birth of Jesus into a pastiche of sentiment, when it was really a story about Holy Wonder.

The essay had been just right for the application to the university that valued deconstructing biblical stories.

Steev had decided when he ran out of time and mental space to repurpose the content of his essay application for the doctoral program for the Christmas Eve homily.

It would do, wouldn't it?

But before the question ever finished forming in his mind, he was shaking his head.

A deconstructed story of Bethlehem was not what people wanted on Christmas Eve.

They wanted the familiar story told the way it had been told longer than he had been alive.

Joy to the world the Lord has come.

Peace and good will to men.

Merry Christmas.

The preacher said the words, but they rang hollow in his own ears, and he figured in what was a growing and very

sobering humility that that was how the congregation would
hear them too.

13

DIXIE IS A GOOD SAMARITAN

When the church parking lot was packed full, Dixie abandoned the responsibility of telling people where to park because she could not figure out where any remaining spot might be. The late comers were on their own. She brushed her hands together. Job done!

Dixie went inside through the side door that the preacher used to come and go privately, passing through a small dark hallway that led to the room where they filled the communion cups and cubed the thick slices of bread that one church lady baked every time they needed it for communion. It was the best bread recipe ever used at the church, but no one knew who the lady was who baked it, so no one could ask for the recipe, which was a shame, because it was a very hearty bread. If you let your little cube of thick bread dissolve on your tongue while you were praying, you could almost taste the ingredients: a wheat flour darkened by a sweetener that was most likely maple syrup or molasses and balanced with a smidge of Kosher salt and enlivened by that fast-working yeast that makes bread rise.

The communion loaves were made in the dear anonymous lady's home and delivered at some time when no one could spot her, but the bread for communion was always ready when it was needed.   And it was the only bread recipe that no one in the church ever complained about.

There had been many a complaint in the past about those small white super-dry cracker chicklets that crunched and bits of which got stuck on your tonsils, or the stale lifeless bread slices broken into bits and pieces and chewed by people who suffered with dry mouth until the grape juice finally was served.

Dixie paused in the communion preparation room. The room where the bread was delivered and the grape juice poured into the small cups was empty—no communion tonight. The absence of it filled Dixie with regret, for she surely loved the Eucharist. It was an astounding event: to physically partake of the healing holy wonder of a Living Savior. She would take it every day if someone would give it to her.

'So be it,' she thought. And then she said aloud, "The church does not work for me. I work for the church."

And upon that rock of repentance, Dixie took another turn through a very narrow door that most people did not see behind the hymn cart that was usually parked there. It was another way in and out of the reception room that was mostly forgotten.

Dixie remembered it.

It was one of her favorite passages from the small hallway into the reception room. She liked to go in there before others arrived so that she could acquaint herself with what was ahead.

Stepping into the room, Dixie was immediately delighted. The ceiling lights were off, and there were candles everywhere. Everywhere. It was romantic and beautiful. Someone had done all of that just for all of them. Dixie's hands went to the middle of her chest where prayer seemed to abide--stored really-- waiting to be released by a gasp of gratitude.

"Oh, thank you," she whispered to all the ladies who had prepared such a vista and to the One who had made the ladies.

Then she saw the other tree. It was smaller and grander in its petite way than the giant tree in the foyer. You had to stand back and look up at that tree in the foyer. This tree in the gathering room could keep you company.

It was only four feet tall and decorated in strings of red and silver beads. Small red bows had been tied here and there as if the tree were a little girl with pigtails that needed bows. Dixie smiled and went to it, taking the edge of a branch between her forefinger and thumb to test if it was real.

It was alive and so wonderfully green.

"I like you better than the giant tree in the other room. You and I could be friends," Dixie whispered. "I even like that there are no lights on you. The natural color of you is pretty enough." Dixie looked down to see if it was standing in a contraption that held water. She did not want the sweet baby tree to be thirsty. Sometimes Dixie could hear a thirsty plant, and she did not want to think this sweet little tree was thirsty. Praises! Someone had filled its water bowl.

Beneath the tree were some wrapped make-believe presents. At least, that is what Dixie thought at first. But leaning down, she could see name tags. Steev. Steev. Steev. Janie. Baby Sam.

Buster. Kathryn. And there were other names she did not recognize.

"Who is Moe?" Dixie breathed. She supposed the names she did not know referred to behind-the-scenes volunteers, and others knew who they were and had left them tokens of appreciation for their service.

Dixie wondered if someone would put a present under the tree for her next year because she was helping with the parking lot. She hoped they would not. It was very difficult to find a good work to do for the pure joy of serving others, and she had found hers. That was enough for her this year and any year to come.

Backing up, Dixie breathed in the fresh aromatic wintry scent of the short, green tree and breathed it out, and in the breathing, she felt that her wordlessness was a kind of prayer that no one had put a name on yet. Her friend Mildred Budge taught her about prayer, but they had not discussed this breathing prayer yet. *Yes, breathing prayers. Glory! Glory!*

Dixie continued to breathe with a holy mindfulness as she moved over to touch the old-fashioned light brown spinet piano. The lid was closed, and there was a sign on it that said: Do Not Open.

The spinet piano was used for smaller funerals. People who died without leaving very many mourners to grieve their absences were funeralized in this room. But at Christmas and throughout the year, receptions occurred here, too, and tonight, in honor of the Candlelight Service there were candles burning in all the windows and on each table. They were wonderful candles and so many of them! They were the battery-operated candles that came on when you twisted the base. How sensitive!

How thoughtful! How intelligent! A real flame so close to children's reach would have been dangerous. No one would have been able to relax if there was a real flame there, and people reaching for cookies.

The ladies of the church had set six round tables decked in alternating green and red table cloths. Large platters of sugar cookies filled each table and, in between the platters, were bowls of nuts and the multi-colored soft butter mints left over from the last bridal shower because the candies were almost out of date, and there was no wedding on the books, so why not place them near the cookies for an extra treat Christmas Eve?

The decision was unanimous.

In two different corners there were drink stands with big bowls of apple cider and pitchers of plain water. The big urns of coffee were percolating still. The aroma was redolent, beckoning.

"So good. So kind. So generous," Dixie whispered, turning slowly to take it all into her heart. "Could life get any better than this?" she whispered, and faintly, just barely, the piano seemed to hum in response. She cast a friendly glance in the humble piano's direction. "It's not your turn tonight," she said. "But stay tuned!" And Dixie laughed.

Then she went to see what needed to be done next to make the Christmas Eve service better for everyone.

14

SILENT NIGHT

One hundred percent of the people who decided to go to the Early Bird Candlelight Service believed that they were going to get a little white candle to ignite and hold while they sang *Silent Night.*

It was only when they got to the door that was the entrance to the sanctuary and looked around for the cardboard box of small white candles they usually took to pass the light of Christ while everyone sang *Silent Night* that they realized somebody had decided that this year they were not going to light any little white candles.

Church members stood in the two main doorways that led to the sanctuary and looked around and thought, *how cozy,* until they realized they were not getting a candle with a little cardboard collar, and then they mumbled:

Where's my candle? Why wasn't I asked whether this was a good idea or not?

Whose bright idea was this? Not to light our candles!

It is not Christmas Eve if we do not light our little white candles and pass the flame from the kid who starts it—the one who gets picked for the honor and who is usually the grandchild of an elder who has been an elder longer than anyone else.

No real candles to light. We did not see this coming, though we should have seen it coming.

They pulled a fast one on us, is what happened.

The same people who decided we only got one chance to go to church on Christmas Eve took away our right to light a candle and sing "Silent Night."

Who is on that Guiding Light Session, and is it time we fired them all?

How much money do you think they spent on those battery-operated candles anyway? The batteries will die before we can use those candles again. What a waste.

After the early irritation subsided, the celebrants found their seats, starting at the front of the sanctuary. The first pews were taken, and as more people arrived, Mildred Budge landed on the fourth pew near the window with a glowing candle.

She was immediately at home.

There, Mildred Budge drifted into a twilight reverie fostered by the muted light from battery-operated candles in the sanctuary. Musing in the muted light caused all the people around her who were whispering about the absence of real candles to grow softer, quieter, and easier to tune out.

Mildred sighed with pleasure. She loved tuning out too much talking, especially in the sanctuary where you could lay aside all the burdens of awareness and focus on goodness and mercy following you all the days of your life.

Mercy was one of the unchanging gifts of the season that lasted year round, but on Christmas Eve, you could take the quiet time in the muted light and the softened chit-chat around you to dwell in it, know it, give thanks for it, remind yourself to remember it, resolve not to create mischief for other people out of idleness and discontent—in short, you could take his yoke upon you and learn from the gentle and lowly One whose yoke is easy and whose burden is light.

People disciplined in meditating explored the features of that rest, but people not trained in meditating could also enjoy the benefits released through the holy wondrous birth of the One who simply changed everything by saying yes to everything his Father asked him to do.

Everything. There is great rest in wearing the yoke of trust.

And you could lay everything down when you thought about that and you were not giving up life itself. You were learning that rest, like memory, has an inherent power to restore and nurture.

Christmas was good for that, too. Any quiet time during Christmas, like sitting in the sanctuary before the service began, was rife with opportunity to experience again that memories and nostalgia were not dead avenues of thinking or being. Memories and nostalgia were portals through which refreshment could come.

Mildred Budge lent herself to the moment as did many other people around her who had, at last, found a quiet place to rest and in the hustle and bustle of a pushing, pulling season let the reality of Christmas and its Holy Wonder overtake every other single thing that was not part of the original nature of a Bethlehem Christmas but pretended to be.

Surrender happened, but no one was embarrassed by it or thought of it in that moment as defeat. Surrendering to the life-giving joy of Christmas is as natural as falling in love or engaging in any other kind of love that is authentic and, in its authenticity, emanates holiness.

All the tightness and the crowded qualities of feeling packed together gave way to ease and comfort and to all kinds of words that pointed in the direction of the truth but were not the experience of truth itself.

Even as Mildred thought the words, Jake was coming toward her. His eyes never stopped smiling. He leaned over and whispered, "Steev needs me to play the piano."

"We will meet you in the cookie room afterwards," she promised.

He nodded, and patted Chase's head.

As he walked back up to the front of the sanctuary she instantly missed him. Missed him. And in the missing, she smiled, for it was an emotion she could both know and not fear. She would see Jake later.

She watched as he settled on the old piano bench. His hands lifted the lid and begin to move across the keys, softly, gently, calling forth a few notes to meet the piano one more time. She knew what he was feeling. She played the piano too. You do not just sit down at a piano and have an instant rapport. You must reacquaint yourself every time with every instrument. That is what Jake was doing as he played a piece of music she could not exactly name but felt she knew.

"I wanted Jake to sit with us," Chase said, leaning into her.

"Me, too," she replied easily, patting his small hand which rested on her forearm.

Jake finished the tune and caught Chase's eye. He patted the place on the piano bench beside him and raised his eyebrows, casting a quick glance at Mildred. She shrugged.

"You can go sit beside Jake if you want to," she said.

And then Jake started to play softly, sparingly, a delicate melody that sounded familiar, but she could not place it immediately.

It was enchanting.

'Emmanuel. Emmanuel.' Mildred could remember only the first two words, and the rest hummed inside of her

Emmanuel. We are with Him and He is with us.

And though Mildred Budge appeared to be sitting alone on the pew without her best friend Fran or her other best friend Belle or her new best friend Jake or her little boy Chase, Mildred Budge was not alone, and when people saw her—and not many took the time to look at her—she was glowing, lit from within, because she was not alone.

15

STEEV LOSES HEART

Looking out at the staring faces in the dimly lit sanctuary, Steev tried to swallow, and the struggle of it made him afraid. 'What if he couldn't preach again?'

Fear triggered a new sensation that other people had described, but it had not happened to him before.

Steev lost heart.

His legs felt wooden.

His good friend over at the piano was trying to smile and nod at him, 'Just keep going, it will get better.'

But Steev could not maintain the gaze of his good friend because he did not believe in that moment that it was going to get better.

The preacher was facing his congregation on Christmas Eve for the first time, and they were expecting his best. He was the master of ceremonies, and he was supposed to conduct that good time.

Unfortunately, the young preacher was gripped in a kind of paralyzing silence. He knew many of the faces out there. He searched for some sign of recognition in them. Friendliness. Encouragement. He looked for Mildred Budge and found her sitting alone on the fourth pew on his right. But she was not looking at him. Her eyes were half closed, as if she were napping, but she did not sleep in church.

'She is praying for me,' he thought. And just the knowledge that someone somewhere was praying for him caused his jaw to loosen. He took a sip of water from the bottle someone had placed on the small shelf below the lid of his pulpit. Water helped. He could swallow again. Words began to form in his mind, and the light that others enjoyed seeing in his eyes—the great friendly light in the new preacher's eyes—began to shine again.

'Our Father, which art in Heaven. Hallowed be thy name.'

It was the preacher's go-to silent prayer when he needed a spark.

But before the preacher could let that spark take hold, a pigeon flew down and landed on the pulpit right in front of him.

The pigeon cooed twice. The sound was caught by the microphone, and everyone heard it.

Silence was filled up by laughter.

Steev laughed, too, expecting the pigeon to fly off.

But it did not.

It held its place on the pulpit and cooed right into the microphone.

When she saw that the pigeon had landed on the pulpit, Mildred thought Jake would do something, but she was wrong. Jake stayed at the piano with Chase.

Instead, an old man wearing pants too big for him moved like a Ninja warrior, stealthily, but faster than you would expect.

Sam Deerborn, who used to make sure the service's special Christmas Eve program was printed for the preacher, walked over to the communion table and peeled the white cloth off it. Carrying that cloth the way a bull fighter prepares to tempt a bull, Sam approached the pulpit; and in a flash of cloth, Sam covered the pigeon and the pulpit with the tablecloth.

Then, inconveniently, the hero of the moment froze.

When dementia patients freeze suddenly there is nothing anyone can do about it. You wait it out, like a fever that just needs to run its course.

The bird was fidgeting under the cloth. The elf who had directed traffic in the parking lot was the only one to see that Sam, the pigeon catcher, though temporarily frozen in place, was loosening his grip on the cloth that confined the pigeon.

The congregation waited; their collective breath held.

"Colonel," Dixie called out. "Colonel Deerborn. Do not let go!"

Sam eyed Dixie in that strange way that he did sometimes when he was trying to remember who someone was.

"Do not let go of that bird," Dixie commanded, holding the door that led to the anteroom where Mark was waiting open with her back against it. She was a sight. Her necklace made of Christmas lights began to blink, and they contrasted with all the muted white-light, battery-operated candles which were positioned around the big meeting room.

Dixie's necklace lights were all kinds of colors, and in that moment of the lit-up, multicolored woman with a fluid personality and an ability to be unpredictably first here and then there, she was helping Sam save the day.

Sam Deerborn would become the unlikely hero of the night again again—no doubt! --as soon as he became unfrozen.

It was just a question of the right motivation, and neither a prod nor a carrot was what was needed: no, neither punishment nor reward.

Instead, Dixie cooed perfectly, mimicking the sound of a pigeon on a window ledge or on a pulpit under a white communion tablecloth.

The whole congregation was mesmerized.

Jake elbowed Chase who grinned. They were having fun.

"This way, this way, this way," Dixie cooed.

At last, Sam heard the pigeon whisperer, and he rotated slowly, holding the pigeon wrapped in the white cloth out in front of him at arm's length like an infant who needed changing, finally attracting the help of a young deacon who had only recently been sworn in with a laying on of hands and had been praying—longing! —to do a good work.

On Christmas Eve, the new deacon was given a good work to do, and he was up for it.

Because the deacon did not know her name, he urged Sam to, "Follow the elf."

And in that short exchange that took no more than two minutes the congregation was realigned, reconfigured, and every one of them smiled. Steev, too.

As the door closed after Sam with the pigeon and the deacon and Dixie, Jake began to play *Silent Night* very quietly, but that melody was only used as an introduction.

Fluidly, Jake rippled lightly into the entrée theme of the children's annual nativity skit, *O Little Town of Bethlehem*.

The door behind which the children were waiting opened, and the players who were going to perform a live nativity filed out, thrilled that the houseful of people were waiting with such bated breath to see them!

See us!

There was Mary. Joseph. The Baby Jesus doll in the manger. Two angels. Three wise men. And one big dog on a leash that was supposed to represent a cow and any other critter who lived in a stable.

The preacher found his voice, and he began, at last.

Gripping both sides of the pulpit, Steev greeted his congregation. "Welcome to Bethlehem."

16

O LITTLE TOWN OF BETHLEHEM

Mark Gardiner had not experienced stage fright in years. But that was because it had been years since anyone had hired him for his voice and stage presence.

His long legs felt wobbly, too.

Mark Gardiner, who could heft a pick ax and use a shovel for hours at a time, had not had jelly legs for longer than he had not had stage fright; but this late afternoon at the church, his legs were shimmying, and it was not from cold or hunger.

Like a chill that causes your teeth to chatter, Mark feared that the jitters were going to work their way up to his hands, and people would see them shaking. If that happened, his voice could begin to waver, and he was likely to sound like Woody Woodpecker. It was the retired actor's first live performance in years, and he was scared to death.

Standing in the wings waiting to go on the stage for the first time in years, Mark envisioned the look on Liz Luckie's face after his comeback, when the man who was presently escorting her from one image-making pose to another was exposed in front of everybody at church as the fraud that he had become over time.

'I didn't used to be a fraud,' Mark promised himself in that small piece of territory that is really you.

'If things go wrong,' he thought, I can say, 'There was no dress rehearsal. The sound system had a defect. And people never recovered from the pigeon incident.'

He had seen the whole pigeon episode and the exit of the old man carrying the pigeon with that lit-up lady who seemed to know her way around the whole building. Those two characters walked right past him in the shadowy anteroom with small nods that barely acknowledged him in the passageway. He did not turn to see which way they went.

He was listening for his musical cue.

And finally, suddenly, jelly legs or not, there it was.

O Little Town of Bethlehem.

His left hand holding the script, his right hand reached out for the wooden banister that stretched up the three big steps that were the same ones the preacher used to reach his pulpit.

But even as Mark took those steps and walked up and past that pulpit, he kept his eyes on the black metal music stand which was his mark.

And as soon as he reached it, a light flickered on. He was no longer standing in the dark.

The audience could see him; but because of the bright light, he could not see them. But he could feel the presence of the smiling lady who stood at the base of the opposing set of steps on the other side of the dais. Even though he could not risk a glance in her direction now, Mark felt the power of Kathryn's smile.

And just knowing Kathryn Harris was smiling at him encouragingly as he reached the black metal music stand and faced the audience, Mark Gardiner smiled.

That was enough.

He was all right again.

Mark tapped on the microphone in front of him and heard the comforting thuds.

Then, he simply began to read the words in front of him, hoping that there was some hint of the timbre of tone in his voice that had once upon a time been his money-making quality.

"And it came to pass in those days that a decree went out from Caesar Augustus that all the world should be registered. The census first took place while Quirinius was governing Syria. So all went to be registered, everyone to his own city.

"Joseph also went up from Galilee, out of the city of Nazareth, into Judea, to the city of David, which is called Bethlehem, because he was of the house and lineage of David, to be registered with Mary, his betrothed wife, who was with child.

"So it was, that while they were there, the days were completed for her to be delivered. And she brought forth her firstborn Son, and wrapped Him in swaddling cloths, and laid Him in a manger, because there was no room for them in the inn.

"Now there were in the same country shepherds living out in the fields, keeping watch over their flock by night. And behold, an angel of the Lord stood before them, and the glory of the Lord shone around them, and they were greatly afraid.

"Then the angel said to them, "Do not be afraid, for behold, I bring you good tidings of great joy which will be to all people. For there is born to you this day in the city of David a Savior, who is Christ the Lord. And this will be the sign to you: You will find a Babe wrapped in swaddling cloths, lying in a manger."

There was a cue on Mark's script to wait for one of the players to speak. But no one did. After an uncomfortable moment, Mark read the player's line.

"A manger is where Jesus slept when no one was holding him."

The congregation murmured. "That is right. That is where Baby Jesus would sleep when no one was holding him."

And all the women who had missed holding a baby remembered what it was like to hold a baby. There was nothing else like it in the world really. Holding a baby dispensed with every kind of loneliness imaginable.

Mark waited. The instructions on his script read: Wait for the chorus to say these words.

Whispers occurred and a couple of giggles.

Then, a group of five women who had been making sugar cookies all afternoon and were now huddled next to Kathryn Harris in the corner by the door, spoke up, loudly:

"And suddenly there was with the angel a multitude of the heavenly host praising God and saying:

"Glory to God in the highest, and on earth peace, goodwill toward men!"

A quick nod to the chorus of ladies, Mark resumed reading while the children waved to their parents when the name of their role was called:

"So it was, when the angels had gone away from them into heaven, that the shepherds said to one another, 'Let us now go to Bethlehem and see this thing that has come to pass, which the Lord has made known to us.'

"And they came with haste and found Mary and Joseph, and the Babe lying in a manger.

"Now when they had seen Him, they made widely known the saying which was told them concerning this Child.

"And all those who heard it marveled at those things which were told them by the shepherds.

"But Mary kept all these things and pondered them in her heart. Then the shepherds returned, glorifying and praising God for all the things that they had heard and seen, as it was told them."

Mark took a breath, and forgetting where he was for an instant, he silently read the words again. *It turned out exactly the way they had been told.* A spark occurred inside the man, and began to warm him in a way that the coat had not. *It turned out exactly the way they had been told.*

When Mark could speak again, he continued reading, his voice mellow and warm. "The Bible account stops here. But the story does not," Mark said, reading on.

"That story unfolded in the life of Jesus, who was real. The Bible tells the truth about him. And those of us who know him must tell the truth about him, too. You can. I can. We all can. Because we have a song of praise to sing every day, and it is not just a carol we sing at Christmas.

"When we accept the reality of the Messiah's birth and all that it means, we can sing Mary's song too. Mary is the mother of Jesus, and she rejoiced when she learned that she would give birth to Jesus.

"Here's Mary's song and when you are a believer, her words can be your song, too."

"My soul magnifies the Lord,
"And my spirit has rejoiced in God my Savior.
"For He has regarded the lowly state of His Maidservant
"For behold, henceforth all generations will call me blessed.
"For He who is mighty has done great things for me,
"And holy is His name.
"And His mercy is on those who fear Him
"From generation to generation.
"He has shown strength with His arm;

"He has scattered the proud in the imagination of their hearts.

"He has put down the mighty from their thrones,

"And exalted the lowly.

"He has filled the hungry with good things,

"And the rich He has sent away empty.

"He has helped His servant Israel,

"In remembrance of His mercy,

"As He spoke to our fathers,

"To Abraham and to his seed forever."

Mark breathed in the hope of goodness and mercy and released his last written line.

"Merry Christmas, friends. Merry Christmas."

"Merry Christmas," the congregation called out good-naturedly, and then they applauded.

Mark's eyes filled with tears. No one had applauded him in years. No one.

The children who had parts in the skit bowed solemnly.

Kathryn Harris signaled to Joseph, who circled in front of Mary, and led the crew of Bethlehem players back the way they had entered.

The Berean ladies who had echoed the words of angels retreated, back to the reception room where they would stand in doorways and help fill cups with apple cider and tell people the secret recipe for making the sugar cookies, which was: "We make them with love. It is the Berean way."

They were the ladies from the Berean Sunday school class, and no one expected a different answer.

17

I'LL BE HOME FOR CHRISTMAS

When you are the wife of a man who has dementia you develop a sixth sense of where to find him when he goes missing.

Belle found Sam standing outside the closed door of Steev's office, and not far away was the hero of the evening—not her husband who had declared that he was going to preach for the preacher, but that Mark fellow, that lover boy who was dating Liz Luckie and who had taken Millie out to dinner before she was keeping company with Jake. Mildred had been quiet about that. Fran had not told Belle much either, saying cryptically long after the unhappy dinner date: "I don't know who to feel sorrier for, Liz or Mark."

And there Mark was standing in the little anteroom, wiping his forehead with a white napkin and looking at her and Sam as if he expected both of them to clap when they saw him.

But neither did. They saw only one another, and this time, Sam reached out to Belle and kissed her on the lips.

It had been ages since her old husband had kissed her. There was no mistletoe hanging overhead. There was nothing she knew of that had prompted the kiss except her arrival.

That was more than enough. Sam recognized his wife, kissed her, and smiled.

"Hello, my Love," Belle said warmly, for his smile was familiar, and in the shadows of the ill-lit passageway, there was a boyish glint to his old eyes.

Mrs. Deerborn felt again why she had married Sam Deerborn and how through the years they had fallen in and out of love and were in a new stage of love now.

"I am so very glad to see you," Belle said.

"I bet you say that to all your boyfriends," Sam replied, with that same glint that she had not seen in more months than she could remember.

Her husband was flirting with her.

Mark was witnessing their reunion when Steev came down the stairs and saw them all standing there.

Sam held out his hand as Steev approached, and Steev understood the way he always did, that Sam needed to shake hands.

He gripped the older man's hand lightly and said, "Thank you, Colonel, for saving us all tonight. You did what no one else could do."

Sam barely heard the words. Instead, the sound of something rustling in Steev's office caused him to turn away. And when he turned back, Colonel Deerborn said to his wife, "Rats in the belfry. Not my problem."

Steev did not raise an eyebrow. "You all right, Belle?" Steev asked, hoping her answer would be a short one.

She reached out for Sam's arm again and tugged gently. "It is Christmas Eve, Steev. All is well, and all will be well. See you later at Mildred's?"

"Hope so," Steev said, and he waited for them to walk off a few steps.

Driven by a desire to be alone, Steev forgot that Mark was standing there, too, opened his office door, and escaped from what others needed of him by going inside his office and closing the door.

The light was off. He stood in his office catching his breath and wondering how long he could hide in there by himself before he had to go to the sugar cookie reception and be the preacher on Christmas Eve again.

18

REMEMBER THE NIGHT

"Mark! Why are you standing in the dark?" Liz rasped in a hoarse whisper filled with accusation. She had walked up onto the stage from the other side and then maneuvered past the pulpit and was now positioned on the top step looking down on Mark.

Holding onto the handrail, Liz descended carefully, trying not to trip in her black velvet high-heel shoes. "You could at least hold out your hand to help me come down these stairs. What are you thinking just standing there like that? Do you know how it looks? Sam does that. You do not want to start acting like a crazy man, do you?"

Mark pretended he did not hear Liz. He was experiencing the fading away of adrenaline and the fatigue that comes from that. And though he had also experienced a mysterious warmth that he wanted to hold onto, he tabled that memory to be relived later. In the moment, he felt tired. He wanted to sit down, but

Liz was not the kind of woman you admitted to that you needed to sit down.

"We can go now," Liz said firmly. "Leave that mess of papers there. Someone will find it," Liz directed, pointing toward his script.

But tired though he was, Mark did not want to let go of those words on those pages. They were warming words and had brought a kind of solace to him that he did not know he needed. Mark wanted to read the words again when he was home alone and see if that same thing happened: that warming. Yes, the words from the Bible had warmed him. And he did not realize how cold he had been for so long. For all his life, maybe. He rolled up the script and slipped it into the side pocket of his new warm coat.

"We can go right through there and show our faces at the reception and then start making our rounds," Liz directed.

"What do you mean--rounds? I thought we were going to Mildred's."

Mark caught a glimpse of himself in a mirror on the wall. It was where the preacher probably checked himself before going up the steps and facing his audience, the congregation. The dark wool coat looked good on him, and Mark smiled at his reflection. He not only felt like himself again; he looked like himself, too. He felt like he was at home in a way he had not felt in more years than he could count.

He wanted to say the words "Merry Christmas" to himself, but they would not come out while Liz was standing nearby. He could not bear the idea that she would hear them and have something to say about it.

"Who knows where the night will take us?" Liz replied coyly. Flirting was her default position when she wanted to get her way.

"Let's go," she directed, moving past him. "I don't know why they won't turn on more lights," she complained. "All these fake candles aren't bright enough."

Liz wended her way through the narrow doorway and ignored the sounds coming from the pastor's office.

Instantly Mark envied that closed door. It was a heavy dark-stained door—real wood.

'What would it be like to have an office with a door you could close and maybe lock?' The idea appealed to Mark as he followed Liz, his hands in his new coat's pockets, one hand gripping the rolled-up script, the other recounting the Tylenols that he needed at home. Four more!

Liz made it to one of the entrances to the reception room and stopped. She often did that before going through a door, striking a pose upon entering a room.

The reception area was a beautifully-lit room with battery-powered candles positioned all around and the overhead light dimmed. People were standing by the several round tables loaded with platters of cookies and other nibbles. In the center of the room was a big coffee pot and an urn with steaming apple cider. Beside the silver urn of cider were bowls containing small cinnamon candies you could add to your drink and sticks of cinnamon supplied as a stirrer. Mark wanted another cup of that warm apple cider and a cinnamon stirrer.

Liz wrinkled her nose and said, "It is not exactly eggnog, is it? Don't worry, Markie. We do not have to stay long."

It was the first time Liz called him Markie, and he loathed it.

"I am not worried," he said, and his own confession surprised him. For on a night that had been fraught with worry and pain, he was not worried. He felt at home.

People he did not know who were sipping cider or coffee called out to him in the friendliest way. They smiled at him, too.

"There you are! The hero of the night."

"Way to go, man. I felt like I was right there with you in Bethlehem."

As Liz led the way, people patted Mark on the back and offered more commentary.

"You saved the day, man."

"Great speaking voice. I could hear you all the way in the back."

"I was up in the balcony, and I heard you. I hope they get you back for Easter."

As if he were accepting an entertainment award, Mark moved through the crowd, receiving the praise, the handclasps; and in the moment, Liz was with him and so a part of that moment— received and welcomed, too. She rotated this way and that, nodding and smiling in Mark's reflected glory, welcome among the brethren who could forget for a little while that she was a serial widow.

"I am with him. Yes, Mark is mine," Liz explained.

For weeks Mark Gardiner had been hoping for just such a moment.

Now. Now when Liz Luckie was saying the words that predicted a financially secure future, he felt cold inside. He did not want to feel cold anymore. Not anymore—not after he had gotten warm and been received so warmly by people who did not judge his clothing or his old, cold house overlooking the river. He thought in that moment that a stable was more comfortable than his tomb of a house that overlooked the river.

Maybe he could sell it after all. Maybe he could sell it "As is." Maybe he would clear enough to buy a small garden home near this church with all these candles burning and so many ladies smiling. He looked for Kathryn Harris and saw her across the room, carrying a platter of cookies and holding them out and motioning, 'Take another one. Take two.'

"Take two," he muttered to himself.

It was the expression a director used when the first take had not been right. Take two. Try again. Yep. There is a second chance.

After you have been to Bethlehem, there is a take two. You can start over. Yes, you can.

Seeing him, Kathryn Harris waved and motioned to him: 'Hold on! I am coming your way.'

Navigating the grazing people, the smiling lady made her way to him.

"I am so glad I found you," Kathryn said, "We will never be able to thank you enough." She had a small, white envelope which she tucked discreetly into the side pocket of the good wool coat where the script was also pocketed.

"Your honorarium," she said. "It is not much, but it is our thank-you. Thank you, Mark," she repeated. "I have got to run. The ladies have rebelled this year, as you may soon find out, Liz."

"Why would I find it out?" Liz asked, mystified.

"Because you are about to see that we did not stick with the traditional sugar cookie recipe this year. We went hog wild," Kathryn Harris announced with a broad grin. "We used all kinds of toppings. Butterscotch. Peanut Butter chips. Rainbow sprinkles. Toffee chips. One recipe for the cookies—a world of flavorings mixed in or sprinkled on top. And we made them all with love. That is our story, and we are sticking with it."

"I like cookies," Mark admitted. It did not feel risky to him to admit that to Kathryn Harris. He would have thought twice about saying the words to Liz for whom an admission like that would have created one weaker place in him she could use against him.

"Eat up," Kathryn advised. And then she paused and studied him appreciatively. "I am so glad that coat fits you. It has been in that closet too long. I hope you can use it."

There it was. Firm agreement. Mark did not stop to feign a response he did not mean. He simply said, "I can use it. Thank you."

"That coat is for a big guy, and you qualify," she said, with a wink toward Liz. Her brown eyes were merry as she whispered something amusing in Liz's ear and then headed back to the ladies in the kitchen.

Mark reached for a cookie, expecting Liz to slap his hand, but she had frozen in space and time just as Sam had before when he was in the spotlight, saving the preacher.

'Everyone is capable of just stopping,' he thought. 'Why do people think it is different when someone diagnosed with dementia does it?'

He took a bite of the cookie. Sugar went everywhere, dusting the front of his coat. 'I can keep the coat,' he thought. 'They gave me an honorarium, as if they honor me.'

"What did she say to you? The smiling lady?" he asked, taking another cookie.

People were getting stacks of cookies and putting them in their pockets and purses or just carrying them in Christmas napkins to the door.

Liz did not answer right away. She seemed to be digesting the words, letting them settle, testing the truth of them.

"Kathryn Harris is nobody's fool," she reported finally.

"That is not what she said," he replied.

Liz turned and looked up at him as if seeing him for the first time. "Kathryn Harris said you were a keeper."

He was warm on a cold night. His toothache was easing. His legs had stopped shaking. And he had eaten those four sandwiches and was feeling better. He stared after the smiling lady,

"She is what Christmas should always feel like," Mark said to himself, but Liz heard him.

She took a second look at Kathryn Harris who threw her head back and laughed, honestly.

"She is just one of those Bereans. Aren't you ready to go yet? I am," Liz said.

Without waiting for an answer, his date led the way to the door that would take them the shortest route to the parking lot.

Mark smiled and nodded to others who spoke to him— invited him to church this Sunday—and he answered readily,

forgetting that his car was only half full of gas, "Sure. I will see
you Sunday."

19

GOING MY WAY

The preacher leaned against the door, closed his eyes, and tried to remember what he had said after the children had performed the nativity scene.

Steev had not given the homily he had prepared. He could not. When he saw the children and looked out at the people who were waiting for him to tell them something about living a life of holy wonder, he could not deconstruct the Bethlehem story. His mouth simply would not open to do that. So, he pressed both hands on top of his prepared remarks and waited to receive something that they needed. It was always a risky choice to make, like taking that first step out onto a tightrope and believing that you could walk across it to the other side without falling.

"God is love." He remembered saying that.

"Jesus is." He remembered saying that, too.

"The Bible tells the truth about him. And you do not really need me or anyone to tell you what it means. To read the Bible is to experience the truth of God is Love and Jesus is. Too." He added that small word, searching and then letting go almost instantly, the need to explain Love. Instead, he released Love in his spirit; and as he released it, he saw Mildred Budge sit up straighter and nod her head, as if she knew what he was doing. In her steady assuring gaze and the nod of agreement, Steev had continued, speaking words he had not planned to say and which had caused the room to go silent. The spirit of the eternal silent night happened in the sanctuary, and the experience had surprised him. One more time.

He had opened his Bible and read Mary's Song again. Slowly.

To his right, Jake nodded, nodded, and though he did not pause long enough to see them exactly, he knew that Jake and Mildred were experiencing Mary's Song in a state of heightened friendship that he did not know with Janie.

Mary's song. It was beautiful. He had forgotten how beautiful. The Bethlehem story hummed inside of him. The idea that a baby was born in a dirty stable made sense to him. That was how faith was born into people with sin-infested lives. Holy Wonder beckons. It is irresistible. You greet Jesus. Then, things start getting cleaned up. You even discover that there is such a dimension to life as holiness.

The adventure of exploring holiness takes hold of you and will not let go even though you fear it will. You are never abandoned, no matter what. Grace after grace happens, and over time, though there are spells of recognizing that a part of you keeps going back to darkness—to hate and lies—you begin to learn that you can always come back to the adventure of holiness. Always return. Seven times seventy. After a while sin as a subject is less interesting to you than holiness. When that happens, the Bible becomes more readily your bread and water, and you begin to partake of a living Christ in ways that are not solely dependent upon the serving of the bread and wine at church. You partake of a living Christ throughout the day and into the night, and over time you grow less afraid that he will call a halt to the giving of himself. You learn that he never stops giving himself to you. When you accept that, fear, like sin, takes a different position in your consciousness.

There is this way to live that is pure and energizing and hopeful. You become not only reconciled to your Creator but reconciled to yourself.

The preacher knew the words. But he was not sure which words he had used after reading Mary's Song out loud and wanting to believe that her message was the homily that the church expected. Needed.

"Maybe next year I will do better," he whispered in the dark of his office.

And then he heard a noise. It was an old building and often creaked, but this sound was different. He listened, tuning in to the direction from which it was coming. He did not have to wait for long. There was a furtive rustling in a pile of papers on the shelf near the window behind his desk.

He knew what it was before he let his hand search the wall for the light switch. One swift brave moment, and there was light. And when he looked in the direction of the rustling papers, he heard a cooing sound before he let himself know the truth.

Perched high up on the top of his bookshelf right above the biographies of famous theologians was that pigeon.

It did not make any sense, and it made perfect sense.

Sam and Dixie had brought the captured pigeon and deposited it in his office. A Christmas gift of sorts. Or, for safe-keeping.

Did the reason make a difference?

He would rather have discovered a dozen notes with requests for his time than to have to catch a pigeon.

And there was no one to call to help him.

Everyone had gone to the sugar cookie reception and would soon be making their slow and winding way to the cars to get to their homes. No one would be in the Christmas spirit enough to want to help him recatch this intruder.

"It is just me and you," he crooned to the pigeon, which cooed in response.

His undelivered homily about a deconstructed Christmas was rolled up in his sweaty hand to be filed for possible future use, maybe. There was a part of him that wanted to swat the bird with his rolled-up notes. Steev paused. There was something in him that wanted to hurt that bird—to kill it, even.

"That's me," he whispered. It was a confession, a prayer. He lived with the echo of the words while he circled his desk, wondering which way would be the best way to approach the bird before it could take off and fly higher. He scanned the ceiling. It could go to the light fixture.

He had to act.

Moving quietly Steev went to his desk, releasing his pages just before grasping the bird, surprised by the heft of the pigeon and the feel of his warmth and the frantic beating of his heart.

He had the pigeon in his hands before he remembered that the office door was closed. Holding the bird with both hands, he could not open the office door. He, like the bird, was trapped inside this space.

He could not make a phone call.

He could not call for help.

"I am at a loss," he said. But the confession was about more than holding the bird captive while he was held captive in his office.

He was just about to let the bird go and open the door and start the whole process again when his door cracked open, and there she was, the elf Dixie who said, her eyes glinting with mischief: "I have come to get my bird."

And then she looked down and saw her bird being held in Steev's hands and grew serious. "He is mine. You do not want him, do you?"

Steev was relieved to see the office door open.

"You haven't hurt him, have you?" she inquired.

And he knew a start of guilt for there had been that moment when he had wanted to swat the bird and underneath that was that other thought that he could wring the bird's neck, put him in the trash can, open the office door, and walk past the cookie-eaters in the reception room and wave as he headed to the dumpster outside. He could almost hear himself saying while smiling his friendly preacher smile, "I will be right back. Just taking out the trash."

"He didn't mean to get in the way," Dixie confided, leaning over. Using her forefinger, she stroked the head of the terrified pigeon. "Preacher will not hurt you," she promised.

"That is right. I will not hurt him," Steev agreed, glad to be coming back to himself in the light by a woman who was a mystery to all who knew her.

"I do not think he wants to live in a cage, so I thought we would just let him go. Let him be."

"Let him be," the preacher agreed. "You lead the way," he urged.

And Dixie grinned, and said, mischievously, "I know a shortcut."

And she did.

She led the way through an unlit hallway he never used down a small passageway that the lady who prepared the communion trays used. "Don't let go," Dixie urged over her shoulder, as she took a right turn and ignored the sounds of people in the formal meeting room.

"I won't," Steev promised, as they reached the foyer with the big tree.

"I like his little brother better," she confessed going past the tall tree.

"So do I," the preacher agreed, though he did not know which little brother she meant.

Then she opened the church door wide and held it for Steev to pass through.

"Sayonara," Dixie breathed, as he released the pigeon.

Dixie watched the bird fly off and asked the question, "Do you think it will snow?"

"Sayonara," Steev repeated softly, watching the bird. And with the bird's flight his own spirit lifted, and when he watched him settle on a tall tree limb, it felt like he was letting go of something he did not know he was holding onto. He stood silently, letting the moment steep within him, until he realized that she had asked him a question. *Do you think it will snow?*

"No, I don't think it will snow," he finally said, but when he looked for her, she was already gone.

There was still only Mildred and Chase standing by their car, and Jake would be joining them soon.

The Christmas Eve service was done. And he began to tell himself the story of it and how he would think about it in the future.

The music had been good. The children's nativity scene was well received. The new reader of the script had a voice any preacher could want. Maybe Mark could be recruited for their Easter program.

He could go to Mildred's house now. He could face what was expected of him there—not just the people, but Janie with the dragonfly tattoo.

But before the preacher could go to Mildred's for Potluck, he had one more telephone call to make.

20

CALLING HOME AT CHRISTMAS

Steev's mother answered the call on the first ring. "Happy holidays."

"Mom, it is me."

"I was waiting for you to call," she said.

Unlike previous years there was no whine in his mother's voice.

It was a different tone of voice than last year or the year before or the year before that. His mother was changing, and her son did not see her often enough or speak to her often enough to know the reasons why.

"How did it go?" she asked politely, for Steev's mother understood that Christmas Eve was a big event for her son the preacher, and Easter Sunday even more challenging.

"Okay," Steev said. "We had a lot of last-minute changes, but there is a lady here who just took care of things. We had a pigeon flying around. The sanctuary was too hot and packed."

He did not add that he lost his way for a while behind the pulpit when he was supposed to know exactly what he was doing—saying. He was the preacher, and he had lost his way.

"You never know what Christmas will bring," she said, but it felt as if her mind were elsewhere.

"How are you and dad?"

"The same," she said. "The people must love you if the room was packed."

He wanted to tell her: It has very little to do with me. I hold a place, but I do not do much more than that.

He wanted to tell his mother about Kathryn Harris and the ladies like her, but his mother would feel that he was implying some kind of hidden message--a judgment against her he did not intend. But he was fascinated by the church ladies who were often overlooked. They were the backbone of church life in this church. Maybe they were everywhere.

"They put the pigeon in my office."

It took her a couple of seconds to respond to that news.

"Was it a joke? Surely they are not playing jokes on you on Christmas Eve."

"The man who caught the bird has dementia. There was another lady—a new lady who was helping him. I will tell you about Dixie sometime."

He wanted to tell his mother more than that. He wanted to tell someone. He could not tell Mildred Budge anymore—not since Janie and he had become aware of each other. Mildred was now on the outside of that—of him and Janie, even though Janie lived with her and he lived across the street from them both.

He was thirsty suddenly and wondered why he had not stopped for a cup of cider or water. It hit him then. He had not appeared at the reception. *Oh, no.* There were probably people waiting there for the preacher still—lingering for one last word with the man whom some believed said prayers that reached God faster and better than the prayers of other people, but that was not true. No preacher had faster or better access to God than anyone else who knew the name of Jesus.

He could not tell his mother that in that moment either. He could not say, "I didn't go to the cookie reception." She would think that he was trying to get off the phone with her, and he did not want to get off the phone with her. It was a paradoxical part of his job: needing to be in more than one place at a time.

He chose his mother, tabling the repentance for failing his congregation that would hit him harder later.

"What are you and dad having for supper?" he asked instead.

"You know your father. He likes Conecuh sausage and pinto beans on Christmas Eve."

"Yes, he does," Steev said, and he could instantly taste the sausage and smell the simmering pinto beans with bacon. In the blink of an eye, he was homesick.

"If you were here, I would make you waffles in the morning with maple syrup. Real maple syrup." There was just a hint of reproach then that he had failed his mom—not come home for Christmas.

"They don't let me off for Christmas," her son explained one more time. He had not been home for Christmas in seven years.

"I bet if I had a medical emergency they would let you off," his mother threatened.

"Don't have a medical emergency," he asked. "I deal with those all the time. Just make the beans and the sausage and watch the Benny Goodman movie you always watch and know that I will come home when I can get there, but it will be a while."

"Your father and I miss you all the time." Her voice cracked.

"I miss you both all the time, too," he said. It was the truth. He could call her every day and tell her that, and it would be the truth, but he did not. He was left with the cliché of the evening. He used it. "Merry Christmas."

"Yes," she replied, for she could not say the words the way he meant them. Not yet.

But as his hand held the phone, something in him took hold as small as a flame on a tiny candle. He believed one day she would. One day his mama would understand Christmas the way he lived it all through the year. *Oh, yes.* That was his unceasing prayer. One day his mama would be able to say what he lived and knew: "Merry Christmas."

2 1

POTLUCK FOR CHRISTMAS

"Jake will be here in a minute, Chase. Are you okay?" Mildred asked.

The boy had grown silent again standing next to the old Mercedes. He was watching for Jake, who was slow to join them. He had said that he had to stop by the kitchen and say good-bye to the cookie ladies who were cleaning up.

"Did you enjoy the Christmas time?" Mildred asked, her voice too bright. She did not sound like herself. She did not feel like herself exactly either. Anxiety hit. There were people coming to the house, and she needed to get home. Belle would be there. Sam, too. Janie with Baby Sam. They would answer the door for her.

"I liked the pigeon," Chase said suddenly.

"Sam and Dixie came to the rescue," she said.

Chase did not react. He was watching the side door of the church—the one that Steev and Dixie had just come through. They had watched as Steev let the pigeon go, and while it happened, Dixie had become motionless, absorbed by the shadows of the encroaching evening.

Chase did not appear to be listening, but he was. He held up a paper napkin with four sugar cookies inside.

"You did not eat your cookies. Are you saving them for later?" Mildred asked.

Surely the boy knew by now that there would be plenty of food to eat at home. He did not need to save cookies.

Chase took his time answering. "Mr. Winston wanted a cookie."

'Did he? Had Winston said that?'

"Did you want to take your cookies to him?" Mildred asked.

The church door opened again, and Jake appeared, lifting a hand in greeting. His other hand was holding a sack of something. He loped across the parking lot, reaching them easily.

"Sorry to keep you waiting," Jake said. "The girls were trying to fold up those tables and take them to the storeroom, and...." He didn't finish his thought. Instead, he said, "What a night."

"It was a good service," Mildred said.

He grinned at her. "That pigeon! Did you see Sam? I did not know the old boy still had it in him. Colonel Deerborn. We must remember that. His title may bring him back to the present moment."

"Chase wants to give Winston his sugar cookies," Mildred said.

"Then he must do that," Jake said firmly. And before she could fret, he smiled and reminded her, "Our friends know how to make themselves at home. Trust that."

"Okay," she agreed simply.

And gone just like that was the anxiety to get home. Everyone could wait. When a boy wants to share his cookies, the whole world can wait. It was important.

Jake's response was warm and immediate.

"That is a good idea. I am glad someone thought of it," Jake said, wordlessly placing his bag of broken sugar cookies on the front seat between him and Mildred. "How was the music?"

"I can still hear it," she replied, smiling.

"Are you buckled up?" Jake asked, looking over his shoulder.

"I liked the bird best," Chase said. The folded napkin with four cookies was in his lap.

They left the parking lot slowly. The last sight they had was of Dixie loading an armful of still shining candles into the basket of her bicycle.

"Where do you suppose she is going with those candles? Mildred mused, though she did not have time to find out the answer.

"We were all supposed to take a candle home with us this year, but that announcement was in the program."

"I didn't get a program," Mildred said

"There was a problem with the programs," Jake said, as they turned toward Winston's house.

"How do you suppose Dixie knew?"

"How does Dixie know everything?" he replied with a question. "She knows her way around that church building better than Steev or me, and she can do it in the dark."

The drive to Winston's house looked different coming from the opposite direction.

More lights in yards and in windows were shining now. People were gathering. Cars clustered around different homes. Silver tinsel on mailboxes caught the moonlight.

The driveway in front of Winston's house seemed lonely, the newlyweds' house still dark.

Jake steered into it carefully, pine cones crunching under the tires. Acorns, too.

"We will just wait for you this time, Chase," Jake said, shifting his hand to Mildred and pressing on her arm. 'Let the boy go.'

"Can you take them to the door by yourself?" Mildred asked anyway.

Chase nodded in the dark. Mildred felt his answer.

They watched their boy walk up to the house. Ring the bell. The door swung open.

Winston was framed in the mellow light of the foyer. He raised one hand to let Mildred know he knew she and Jake were there. And then he leaned over slightly and held out his open hand for his Christmas cookies.

Standing in the mellow light, Winston smiled; and when he did, it became a merrier Christmas.

22

MILDRED'S HOUSE
ON CHRISTMAS EVE

At Mildred's house, Belle and Colonel Sam Deerborn were already inside, making themselves the host and hostess until the lady of the house returned.

The baked ham was resting on the kitchen table, partially sliced. Once the platter that held the ham grew empty, whoever was nearby would slice some more meat. No one complained or looked about for someone who could use a carving knife. Friends of Mildred on Potluck Night just made themselves at home. Useful, too.

Organized by Belle, large cookie sheets of biscuits right out of the can (two cans for five dollars) were being baked and coming out in twenty-minute intervals. The buttermilk biscuits were big and piled in serving bowls with saucers nearby containing sticks of butter.

The message was clear for Potluck at Mildred's.

Help yourself.

Do you like a lot of butter or a little or none?

A little maple syrup goes with baked ham. Yes, it does.

Oh. That brown twig? That is a clove. You do not eat them, but you can chew on them. They are good for your breath.

Four precious jars—two each of pear preserves and glorious cherry preserves --were on the small table where Mildred and Chase ate their breakfast. These had been sent by Uncle Jody and Aunt Julie, but no one was sure whose aunt and uncle they were. They just made fruit preserves in the late summertime and sent them as gifts to special people for the holidays. The recipient had brought them to share because hot biscuits needed preserves, and it was Christmas. You share your best at Christmas.

"Everything okay in here?" Mildred asked, coming in the back door. The kitchen was a mess, and she loved it.

Pulling back a long piece of tin foil from a large serving dish, Belle announced, "It's truly Christmas. We have got apple cheese again."

"Moe?" Mildred confirmed.

Belle nodded seriously. "Moe's apple cheese."

"Apple cheese," Mildred sighed. It was the most delicious concoction of peeled and slice apples marinated in a sugary syrup and topped with melted cheese that was slightly browned and crusty. Delicious taste. Delicious texture! It was Christmas when Moe's apple cheese appeared at a Potluck.

"I am going to get comfortable, Belle. Are you all right in here?"

Belle shrugged. She could handle the arrival of covered dishes with one hand tied behind her back, blindfolded. She replied, "I'm going to put some of this apple cheese in two of those plastic containers and hide them in your fridge. One for you and Jake, one for me and Sam."

"Get us a lot," Mildred said, as she walked off down the hallway to her room to freshen up as she heard the doorbell ring and the front door opened. She tried not to look at Janie's room, but the girl's bedroom door was open. The girl was gone. Dirty clothes were in a pile by the closet. The smell was unpleasant. A tall trashcan near the baby bed was packed full of soiled diapers.

If Mildred went in there and got the trash bag and took it outside to the big can, Janie would feel judged.

Mildred closed the bedroom door, a compromise solution. That would have to do. She had to live with Janie. Maybe her guests would not notice.

The doorbell rang, and Mildred kept walking toward her room and a few minutes of quiet before conversation was expected of her.

Belle would get the door. Or Sam. Or anybody standing near it.

She heard Liz and Mark arrive and went into her bedroom and closed the door. She sat down on the edge of her bed, kicking off her good shoes. Then, she caught a glimpse of herself in the mirror over the bureau and advised, "Hold on. You can do it."

Then she said the words she would soon be repeating to others, "Merry Christmas."

She remembered Winston's face when he leaned over and took the sugar cookies from Chase, and she smiled and said the words again.

23

AT HOME ON CHRISTMAS EVE

No one kept count of who came and went at Mildred's after the Christmas Eve service. Many friends entered through the back door, or depending on where they parked in the street walked across the front lawn to her front door. Purses and jackets were stacked here and there, sometimes on the small telephone table near the front door or behind a larger chair in the living room on the floor. Covered dishes were taken to the kitchen or if there was an empty space on the dining room table, simply placed there with the called out request, "Where can I find a serving spoon?"

Most people forgot to bring a big spoon with them, but that was all right. Mildred Budge had plenty of big spoons stored in a nice jar on a counter near the coffee pot.

Once they were settled, friends began making plates. Christmas at Mildred's made you hungry. and often, once they had fixed a plate or simply made a ham biscuit and carried it around in their napkin to eat while they talked to friends, they went outside and sat on one of the outdoor chairs or in the new metal glider that was just right for two people who wanted to catch up in private.

Janie used that glider for rocking Baby Sam for his afternoon bottle.

But on Christmas Eve, people kept each other company there, needing some time alone with someone else who could read their minds when the words they wanted to say would not come.

Conversations were intimate, appearing to be made up of tidbits of talk, but the tone was reverential.

"The cookies were good. What was different about them this year?"

"Kathryn Harris would know. She oversaw the cookie brigade this year."

"They are going to wear her out one day."

"Bereans do not wear out. They just ride off into the sunset."

The gentle rocking motion of the glider often took hold in the middle of conversations and the back and forth movement of the unselfconscious conversation eventually faded away, and became only two quieted people gliding under the stars, keeping each other company on Christmas Eve—sleeping in their own beds ahead of them, but they were not in a hurry to get there.

After a while they moved along and another pair of old friends took their time in the outdoor glider under the stars and another conversation commenced, ruminative and harmless, an easy back and forth of releasing observations that wasn't gossip or malice.

"What do you think is going on with Mildred and Jake?"

"Nothing."

"How can you be so sure?"

"Because Mildred Budge is single, and she is old enough to have gotten married. If Mildred had wanted to get married she would have by now. Nothing is going to happen there."

"Do you think that is what Jake wants?"

"He is a mystery man."

"It is funny how a woman staying single all her life is just an old maid, but a man who is single is a mystery man."

"You want something sweet to eat?"

That last question caused the glider riders to rise and wiggle through the small opening of the metal glider and make their way back into the kitchen through the sun porch for another portion of a Elsie's chocolate delight or a blondie with butterscotch chips or another taste of Moe's famous apple cheese.

Instinctively, they kicked their shoes off now, for they had walked through the grass, and they did not want to track Mildred's kitchen floor.

***

The food on the countertops accumulated as more people arrived and were changed out for the dishes that had already been emptied. The countertops were loaded with all kinds of offerings. Friends brought jugs of maple syrup, quarts of potato salad from the Publix deli, and even though they knew Mildred was serving a big ham, they sometimes brought a tray of deli meats. These were placed on the dining room table when a serving platter became empty.

When the tall kitchen trash can began to overflow, the last person to try and stuff a napkin in it snagged the red-pull ties, lifted the full bag out, and carried it to the big rolling trash can outside near the back door.

A person left behind in the kitchen mused softly out loud, "Where does Millie keep the trash bags?" and someone else said, "The cabinet nearest the trash can."

And there they were.

"How did you know that?"

Because it makes the most sense: keep stuff near where you need. That's Mildred Budge.

Conversations rumbled but they were just ruminative and more curious than anything else.

"What is she going to do with all this food?"

"It is not going to fit in her refrigerator."

"She will pass it on to Belle and Sam. Belle cannot cook much, and Sam's a big eater. The preacher lives across the street. He will get some of it."

"There is Fran and Winston, and Fran's not cooking right now."

"She won't take this food to them."

"No, she would not. Fran's appetite is off. I wonder how Winston is doing."

When Mildred came out of her bedroom, she stopped in the hallway and listened to the voices coming from various rooms in her small bungalow.

The kitchen people were louder and standing while they talked.

The living room people were the more formal guests, who were perched on folding chairs and the remaining sofa.

The people in the living room were the ones who still used a plate and worried about placing a cup on the top of the table for fear it would leave a ring.

Liz and Mark were in the living room. When Mildred passed through she saw Liz settling her handbag on the floor between the side table and the long sofa against the wall.

Mark looked uncomfortable. He was sitting strangely upright and on the edge of the sofa.

"Do you want to take off that coat?" Mildred asked.

She pointed toward a coat rack, which was loaded with garments. Purses were piled beneath it. Occasionally a cell phone in a purse buzzed, but no one hurried to find out who was calling. *It could wait.*

"Everything is all right, Millie," Kathryn said. "Why don't you get yourself a plate?"

Mildred nodded, becoming a guest of sorts in her own home. She looked around for Chase and Jake.

"They are in the glider having a talk," Kathryn said, reading her mind.

"Good," Mildred said. She went to the kitchen and surveyed the mess. It was her favorite kind of mess. Food everywhere. Paper plates and disposable cups stacked where she had placed them. There was a cooler with ice. On the kitchen counter were two bottles of champagne. She placed them in the bottom drawer of the crisper in the refrigerator.

Mildred heard Kathryn making the rounds. "Need anything? Liz? Do you know where things are?"

Mildred stopped to hear Liz's answer. She could not make out the words.

"Mark, thanks again for pitching in for us tonight. What can I get you?"

Liz's voice grew louder. Mildred smiled.

"I am going to make us a plate to share," Liz said. "We do not want much. Just some nibbles."

"Why don't you both make your own plates? There is a lot of food," Kathryn suggested.

"We do not need a lot of food. We are not hungry," Liz said firmly.

"Mark, why don't I make you a plate and Liz can make her own?" Kathryn offered. Making someone else's plate came second-nature to her, as easily as choosing small portions did. Hers was a lifetime of avoiding gluttony, not weight gain.

"You do not have to do that. I can make him a plate if he wants one. Do you want your own plate?" Liz asked, waiting for Mark to accede to any plan she preferred.

He nodded yes instead.

"I will make you a plate, darling. I know how to make a plate," Liz declared emphatically. "You can talk to him while I'm gone," Liz told Kathryn.

Kathryn smiled tolerantly. But it was a different smile than the famous Kathryn Harris smile. It was a gentle and lowly smile that assured Mark that his vulnerabilities were safe with her.

Kathryn ignored Liz's directive and said, "I am going to get you a ham biscuit," she said.

It was a short walk from the living room to the dining room table and the pile of biscuits with ham. She nabbed two and brought them to him on a small paper plate. "It's not Christmas Eve if you don't have one or two of Mildred's ham biscuits."

Mark cast a quick glance at the door that Liz had taken to the kitchen and took a big bite. Three bites into it, Mark relaxed, his eyes closing slightly, as hunger pains abated.

Liz had gone to the kitchen and had chosen a single nine-inch paper plate, looking around for something to put on it. What a mess. She did not know how Mildred could stand all this food all over her kitchen.

24

DINNER NEXT YEAR?

"Do you want to have dinner sometime next year?" Mark asked Kathryn while Liz was in the kitchen.

It would have to be in the new year after his social security check had been deposited.

"No, thank you," Kathryn replied simply, nodding at other guests. She had made a mistake giving him biscuits. It was hard to be hospitable and not make a mistake with a single man. It was an unspoken plight for many church ladies that their desire to feed others often caused the hungry person to mistake the offering of food for something else.

"We could take a river cruise," Mark proposed, stretching his arm across the back of the sofa. The river cruise was very affordable. He let his fingertips touch Kathryn's shoulder blade. It was a silk blouse. Silk spelled money. He smiled knowingly at her.

Kathryn blinked at his touch and shifted to the right. Mark's knowing smile caused her to grow cold.

"Montgomery is pretty when you look at it from the water," he confided.

"I know how Montgomery looks from every angle," Kathryn said. She recalled that her good friend Mildred had gone on a dinner date with this man before he began dating Liz, and she knew that Mildred had stopped seeing Mark afterwards. She didn't know anything else, but that was enough to know.

"But you haven't seen Montgomery with me," Mark explained. He leaned toward her, fixing his gaze upon hers. "I don't think you will be disappointed."

"Disappointed about what?" Liz demanded to know.

She was carrying only one small plate of food after all, and there was a moment when Kathryn thought Liz was going to throw it at them. Kathryn repositioned herself to get out of the line of fire.

"I got us some very nice celery and carrot sticks and that is hummus. I was surprised to see hummus. I like hummus."

"Hummus," Mark repeated, looking down at the plate. "I am more of a meat man," he explained, lifting the second ham biscuit, and taking a bite.

He chewed while Liz studied him. When Liz sat back down beside him, she did not move closer. Instead, she perched on the edge of the sofa and dipped a carrot stick in the hummus and took a mincing bite. She ate it like a rabbit nibbled at food, and Mark thought, 'I don't like rabbits in the yard.'

2 5

MILDRED'S CHRISTMAS EVE
HAM BISCUITS

"How big was that ham?"

"I think Mildred said it was eighteen pounds."

"And she did not put anything on it? No glaze? No orange marmalade? No pineapples and brown sugar?"

"Nope. Mildred said all she did was put cloves in it, and Chase did that. Mildred said he had quite a knack for putting cloves in the ham."

"Makes the house smell good."

"That is the biscuits baking too."

"Did Janie bake those?"

"I don't think so. It is hard to watch an oven when you have a baby."

"Janie is outside in the front yard talking to Steev."

"I thought that was her, but I was not sure. When I arrived, Steev waved at me to go on, and they walked across the street to his yard. I think they are sitting on his front porch now."

That news traveled quickly around the room.

"The preacher is keeping company with the young girl living with Mildred Budge. She has that baby. Well, that would not be the worst thing to happen to a man who needs a wife. A preacher needs a wife and a family."

"He could do worse than marry an instant family. No, that is not a bad idea."

About eight o'clock Baby Sam's cry from Janie's room quickened a response from Belle who had been listening for the sound of the baby named after her husband. She went to Janie's room and gathered the baby boy to herself and sat down in the small rocker Mildred had inherited from her grandmother. It was compact and sturdy.

Kathryn followed Belle, asking automatically, "Does Baby Sam need a change?"

"Yes, I will do it in a minute."

"Where is Janie?"

"Outside talking to Steev."

"Do you want me to heat up a bottle?"

"Someone should," Belle said, and she settled until Kathryn brought the warmed formula and stood in the doorway while Baby Sam settled in Belle's arms. The two women listened peacefully to the baby's gurgles and to the other lullabies, the nearby sounds of people in the den and the living room and the kitchen as they began to take their leave and head home for what was not an early night for them. Most of the people in

Mildred's house went to bed around nine o'clock, so they were just following their routine.

"That was a nice service," Kathryn remarked in a whisper.

She was not making a judgment. She was making conversation.

"It always is," Belle replied amicably.

Taking care of her husband had changed Belle. She had very few negative opinions about anything at all anymore. If you were part of a crowd, chances are mistakes were being made because people were human, and they excelled at making mistakes.

"I was able to sit through the whole service," Belle said, repositioning the bottle for Baby Sam.

"We had enough cookies for everyone," Kathryn said. She was not bragging. She was reporting a fact.

"Aren't you tired?" Belle asked, looking up.

"I really am."

"Then sit down."

"I don't want to sit on her bed."

Belle nodded. Sitting on someone else's bed was an infringement.

"You do not have to stay in here with me. You can go back out there. I am fine."

"Do you want me to check on Sam?" Kathryn asked.

Belle shook her head. "I am not worried about Sam. He is like a homing pigeon." And saying that, she laughed. "Did you see my old man catch that bird?"

"I did not," Kathryn said. "I heard about it though." She paused before adding, "I think that Mark is hungry."

"I was thinking that too," Belle admitted, holding the bottle. Baby Sam gurgled. His mama was out in the front yard in the dark talking to the young preacher. "I was thinking we might put together a to-go bag for Mark."

"I can make the bag, but I can't be the one to give it to him," Kathryn said.

Belle studied her and nodded knowingly. "No, you should not do it. He likes widows."

"That's what they call me now," Kathryn agreed. "But I am still married. My sweetheart just is not here anymore."

"I know exactly what you mean," Belle replied easily.

The two old friends smiled at one another.

"I don't want Mark to be hungry," Kathryn said.

"But you don't want him," Belle said, tipping the bottle higher so that the formula came out more easily.

"I would rather eat hummus and carrot sticks, and I don't like hummus—though I do like carrots," Kathryn agreed easily.

"What if when I finish here I put together a to-go bag. Mildred has some canvas totes from the grocery store, and we can just hand it to him when they start to make their exit. What can Liz say if we do that? More important, what can he make of that?"

"I will put the bag of food together and place it by the hat rack at the front door. If you finish in here in time, you could hand it to him."

Belle nodded that she had heard. "This is a sweet baby," Belle said, watching his face. "Do you need to hold him?"

"No," Kathryn said. "I will go make that to-go bag. I will make two. I will bet you there is somebody else out there who would like to wake up to a biscuit and a slice of ham."

"Why don't you make one for yourself and me?" Belle called after her.

And with the question, Kathryn laughed. She nodded yes as she walked back out into the hallway, taking a turn away from the lingering guests seated all over the house but most relaxed in the den with some people sitting cross-legged on the floor because the chairs and sofa were full.

In the kitchen, Kathryn surveyed the vast amount of remaining food and wondered what a bachelor who could not cook would be able to manage. And then, she packed up some ham slices, some unbuttered biscuits, and a jar of camp stew that had been brought but not been opened. There was a quart of unopened orange juice and a pint of carrot salad not tapped. She packed those, too.

It did not take long to fill a bag. Then she filled another. And another and placed them all at the front door. Then she made another to-go bag for Sam and Belle and placed it on the porch by the back door that led to the field and their house. Belle would find it.

By then it was very dark outside. The stars were bright; and though they would all have enjoyed some snow, the sky was clear.

Peering out, Kathryn saw the glider was empty. It was her turn now. Kathryn walked out and sat down in the glider. She thought of her husband while rocking in the glider and let the sounds of the people inside subside, giving way to a Christmas moment that was all her own. She spoke softly to the shadows.

"I got through another one, and now there is only New Year's Eve, and I will get through that too. I miss you all the time," she said, and she rocked gently, alone in the glider, wondering how long the others would stay inside talking and eating before they decided to go home. "By the way, you bought an awful lot of Betty Crocker sugar cookie mixes. But it was a buy one, get one sale. That was your Christmas present to me and everyone else at the Church on the Corner, and we all loved it."

26

AND TO ALL A GOOD NIGHT

When Janie came back inside the house, the baby had fallen asleep and was safely in his crib.

Belle had brought out the trash bag of soiled diapers and wordlessly settled it on the back stoop. She would take it to the big outdoor trash can when she and Sam headed home across the open field to their own house in Cloverdale.

Most everyone had already left. Just a few people lingered.

The awkwardness of arrivals and the bright chatter from being Christmas visitors had faded to the sounds of close friends just saying *so-long. Merry Christmas.*

Parting gifts were offered from the two big cardboard boxes of fruit—one by the front door and the other on the back porch. Friends of Mildred Budge and Jake Diamond were urged to help themselves to a little taste of sunshine.

"Grab an orange from that box on the front porch. Take a grapefruit. They are Indian River. The Boy Scouts are selling them again this year."

At the front door, Liz fluffed her collar and looked around for Mildred but did not see her. "We can just leave," Liz told Mark. "Millie doesn't care if we say good-bye."

Mark shook his head. "We need to say good-bye and thank you," he said firmly. He was feeling stronger since he had eaten. He was warm. The throbbing tooth had eased considerably.

Inside the house again, Kathryn saw that Mark and Liz were ready to go. With Belle nowhere in sight, Kathryn signaled to Mildred, *come help me get them out the door.*

Church ladies read each other's minds all the time.

Mildred headed to the front door.

"So glad you could come, Mark. You were great tonight reading that script. Thank you for the jar of dill pickles, Liz," Mildred said.

"They are good for weight control," Liz explained. "When you feel like eating sugar, Millie, eat a dill pickle instead. It is how Joan Crawford kept her weight down. It worked for her!" Liz said the words easily.

Mildred smiled. "I will remember that," she said, holding the front door open. It was a beautiful evening, and it had been a wonderful night.

"Thank you, Millie," Mark said. He wanted to lean over and kiss her on the cheek. From where he came from, you kissed people good-bye; but in the South, people hugged instead.

Before he could figure out what to do about it, Belle suddenly appeared and reached down for a to-go bag. "Mark, we are trying to clean up the kitchen. We need help with the overflow of leftovers. Will you please take some left-overs home? Have you got room in your fridge? Please say yes," Belle asked.

"Yes," he said simply. "Happy to help."

"You keep saving the day," Mildred said, eyeing Mark warmly. He seemed different. Better.

Liz reacted.

"Well, come on then," Liz said, urgently. "It is getting late for these people. Do not tell me you are an early birder," Liz warned Mark. And grabbing his arm, she claimed, "We are night owls."

Mark stifled a yawn and said, "Speak for yourself, Liz."

Liz looked up at him sharply. Mark had changed. Up until this moment he had simply agreed with her. Something had happened. Mark was not automatically agreeing with her anymore. She eyed Mildred Budge sharply—her competition.

"Did you get an orange?" Mildred asked Liz.

"I don't need an orange," Liz replied stiffly.

Mark opened his bag and said, "I would love an orange for later."

Mildred placed two in his well-packed to-go bag. "Rest well," she said. "So glad you could come."

Jake appeared behind her then. "Are we saying good night?"

"No rush," Mildred said, though she hoped the others would leave soon.

The baby had settled. The kitchen was still a mess. The dining room, too.

She saw Kathryn heading toward the kitchen. "Kathryn, do not even think about cleaning up that kitchen. It can wait. You have done enough today. Go home. Get some rest."

Kathryn stopped and nodded. "If you say so."

"Go home. Get some rest. Take some food with you."

"I made myself a to-go bag. But I didn't know about the fruit here. I would like an orange and a grapefruit," Kathryn said. But before she reached for the fruit, she said, "Let me find my purse." *Where had she left it? Behind that chair. Yes, and there it was.* She peeked inside at her cell phone. *No messages. Good.* And disappointing too. After a barrage of texts and phone calls, the silence was welcome.

While Kathryn was retrieving her purse, Mildred found a plastic sack and placed two oranges and two grapefruits in it for her friend.

Jake took Mildred's hand while she stood in the doorway and waved good-bye to all who were leaving, slowly, sleepily, lingering out in the street by the cars under the moonlight, continuing conversations that might have begun in the glider or elsewhere and which were still not quite finished being told.

When the last car had eased away slowly toward home, Jake looked down at the mostly empty fruit box. "The Boy Scouts came through."

"It was a good evening," Mildred said. "I missed Fran and Winston though."

"They are not far away, and there is the new year. I think it is going to be a very a happy one," Jake predicted. "Are we cleaning up tonight?"

"Just the stuff that needs to go in the fridge."

"Everything else can wait," Jake agreed.

"Is Chase...?" she asked.

"Asleep in his clothes on his bed. He is fine."

She nodded, feeling herself want to sink onto the nearest chair. But there was so much to do. Christmas Day was next. Church two days later. She had a Sunday school lesson to prepare though attendance during the holidays was usually thin in Sunday school.

"Do you want a glass of champagne?" Jake asked, and then shook his head. "I forgot to chill it."

"I found champagne and put it in the fridge earlier," she said.

She thought about squeezing some oranges and having mimosas, but she did not want to work that hard. "Champagne sounds good," she admitted.

Her brown eyes sparkled in the muted lights, and Jake thought she looked like one of those ladies that the old master painters used to capture with their oils and portrayed in quiet settings of dignified chairs and velvet curtains behind them.

"By the tree?" Jake suggested. "I wouldn't mind some quiet time before heading home myself."

Before Mildred could agree, Sam appeared.

"Is the party just starting?" he asked.

"There you are," Mildred said, smiling. "Where have you been all night? I have missed you."

"That's your problem," Sam said, hitching up his pants. "I can't be everywhere."

"Where is Belle?" Jake asked. If Belle appeared, maybe she could steer her old husband home and he and Mildred could relax with their champagne.

Sam looked quizzical. "Belle?"

"Belle," Mildred repeated.

Janie appeared suddenly. Her hair was a mess and her eyes were red from crying. "Could you people hold it down?" she asked angrily. " I have finally gotten the baby to sleep."

It was the first time Mildred had seen Janie close enough to talk with all evening. She had heard about the outdoor discussion with Steev on the front lawn. He had not come inside, and Janie had not joined the party when she returned. Mildred had thought Janie might have retreated to the glider, but when she had looked for her, she saw only Kathryn Harris, rocking quietly, lost in the kinds of thoughts you do not disturb.

"Where have you been all night?" Mildred asked. The question sounded accusatory, but she did not mean it that way. She wondered why the girl couldn't enjoy the fellowship of her friends—such sweet friends.

"Talking to Steev outside," Janie said, and a veil crossed her face. "I have got to find a new job. The program for tonight's service wasn't good enough apparently, and people didn't take all of those expensive candles home because they didn't see the announcement about it because they didn't give out the program, and that's somehow my fault, though Mister Steev himself could have said something about the blamed candles up on the stage while he was talking, but he didn't, and now I have got to find a new job. He gave me a month's notice," she said, and turned and stomped back to the bedroom past the small Christmas tree under which there were already a considerable number of presents.

People had slipped small gifts under the tree without making much of an issue about it. A lot of them had the name Chase written on them. Others had Little Mister, the name the ladies had called Baby Sam before he was born.

Mildred did not immediately see any new gifts for Janie, and that saddened her. But the ladies had not warmed to Janie since she had moved in.

'Here you all are," Belle said, appearing as Janie left. "The kitchen is all right, Millie. All the stuff that needs to be refrigerated has been put away or given away. The kitchen will hold until tomorrow. That ham was good."

"People seemed to like it," Mildred agreed contentedly. "You need to sit down, Belle. You have been going pretty hard all day too."

"I would like to sit down," Belle agreed, taking a place on the other end of the small couch. It was a place that Jake had been expecting Mildred to be—to join him.

He rose. "We are about to have some champagne. I will get more cups," Jake offered, with resignation.

It was almost ten o'clock—an hour past Mildred's regular bedtime.

When Jake returned and everyone had a paper cup of champagne, Sam said loudly, "How about a toast?" and before anyone could offer one, he said, very loudly, "Ho-Ho-Ho."

Janie came back out and glared at Sam. He tipped his glass toward her as Baby Sam began to cry loudly in his room.

"You can bring the baby out here if you want to," Belle invited.

Janie stomped off back down the hallway. Baby Sam continued crying. Janie did not come back out. A few seconds later they heard her in the kitchen warming more formula.

Belle wanted to tell her, "I gave him a bottle at eight," but Mildred shook her head. *Let her be.*

"Does anyone know what happened to Dixie?" she asked instead.

"There is a stocking for her up there," Mildred said, pointing.

A line of packed red velvet Christmas stockings hung from her fireplace. The names had been written on each one at the top of the stocking in black marker, and true to a retired school teacher's habits, the stuffed stockings were hung alphabetically.

Belle. Chase. Dixie. Fran. Jake. Janie. Mildred. Sam. Steev. Winston.

"That is very sweet," Belle remarked. "I haven't had a stocking in years."

"Just chocolate kisses and peppermint sticks—the kind that melt easily in your mouth," Mildred said.

"I like chocolate kisses. Silver bells," Belle said, looking at her husband who had drained his glass of champagne. But he did not seem to want more. If she did not take him home soon, Sam would fall asleep on the sofa. Belle thought about that— thought, *I could just let it happen. Mildred would be all right.* And then Belle thought about the boy waking up and coming out and finding Sam before he saw the presents from Santa, and she said, "Old man. It is time to go home."

Sam did not rouse.

"Old man," Belle repeated.

Sam did not respond.

Jake leaned over and tapped Sam gently on the knee. "Colonel Deerborn. The lady is talking to you. She needs you to walk her home."

"Well, why didn't you say so?" Sam said, rousing and eyeing Belle curiously. "I like fat women," he said. It had been a while since they had discussed her weight, but the memory resurfaced.

Belle walked over and stuck out her hand. Sam gripped it, and she helped lever him to his feet. "You need anything else before we go?" she asked Mildred.

Janie finished in the kitchen and stomped back to her room, signaling the message-- *All of you go home.*

"Get some rest," Mildred said. "Did I see a to-go bag for you by the back door?"

Belle nodded. "Kathryn made it."

"Weight in gold," Mildred breathed, taking another sip.

"Price above rubies," Belle agreed.

"She is a spectacular woman," Jake said suddenly. "You should have seen her in the kitchen earlier. And then the skit. She was the one who recruited Mark to narrate."

Belle looked up sharply from Jake to Mildred, who simply said, "Kathryn is quite wonderful. Just wonderful. No job too small or too hard."

"Spectacular," Jake approved, taking a sip of his drink.

"Do you want your stockings tonight?" Mildred asked, settling down on the piano bench. She didn't want to crowd Belle.

"We will get them tomorrow," Belle said. "Everything was good. It always is."

"I never do it alone. That's how I can do it," Mildred said, mouthing the words quietly, *thank you, Belle.*

"I like fat women," Sam repeated, but this time he was looking at Mildred.

Mildred smiled up at her good friend who in his peculiar way was making an effort to get along with others. "Mind how you go, Colonel Deerborn."

"But I don't like women telling me what to do."

"He really doesn't," Belle said, taking his arm. "Would you walk me home?"

He eyed her in the shadows of the room as she took his arm and began to steer him toward the kitchen to the back porch where they would grab a to-go bag and walk across the back field to their home.

Mildred followed them to the back porch, watching as Belle steered her husband, taking careful steps in the shadows under the moonlight along a well-worn path from Mildred's to their back door. They picked up the bag of trash and took it with them, stopping to put it in the big can before walking on.

"That was the last of them," Mildred said, going back to the den. The room was quiet—the air settling. Baby Sam had stopped crying. Janie, too.

"Did you like the ham?" she asked.

Jake did not answer right away.

Jake was finally all alone with Mildred Budge. He patted the place on the sofa where Belle had been and sat back, feeling the fatigue of letting go. But content, too.

"I don't know what happened to Dixie. I don't think she ever came here," Mildred mused, taking her cup of champagne. It looked pretty when the lights from the tree caught it. Magical. Romantic.

"I saw our Dixie leave the church holding an armful of those shining candles from the sanctuary. She said Kathryn gave them to her because she liked them so much. Kathryn seems to always know what to do," he said, taking a swallow. The champagne was burning his stomach, and he set his cup aside.

"She had a bicycle. I offered her a ride, but she said that she had someplace to go, and besides, she said, if it snows, she wanted to see the first snowflake that falls."

It had been a long time since snow fell in Alabama.

"Sometimes I envy Dixie," Mildred admitted. "I hope there are some oranges left. I would like to squeeze some for Chase tomorrow. I bet he has never tasted freshly squeezed orange juice."

"That's tomorrow. This is tonight," Jake said firmly, taking Mildred's cup.

"I don't think I want anymore," she said. "It is kind of late for me to drink champagne."

Before Jake could explain that refilling her cup was not what he was thinking, the phone rang.

Instantly, she stood up. "Who could be calling at this hour?"

"Do you have to answer it?" Jake asked, but she did not hear him.

She answered the phone on the second ring and knew the caller instantly.

"Fran, are you all right?" Mildred asked. Her heart began to race. *Trouble. Trouble.*

Her left palm instinctively went to her chest. "Uh-huh. Uh-huh. Yes," Mildred said before hanging up.

"Fran ate one of Winston's cookies. Fran ate a cookie," Mildred repeated. "And she thought it tasted good. She was calling to say thank you."

That was the kind of phone call that could have waited until the next day. But Jake did not say anything. Fran and Mildred were close. He wondered if he would ever be as close to Mildred as she was to all of her long-time friends.

"That means that Fran is getting her appetite back," he said, settling down in what was now his place on the den sofa.

Mildred beamed. "That wasn't all she said. It seems that Dixie rode on her bike over to their house and put all of those lit-up candles on their front porch. Fran was thrilled. Thrilled."

"The light of Christ," Jake said, leaning his head back. It had been a long day. A long good day. He was ready for Mildred to be at home with him, but she was reliving the triumph of the sugar cookies and now the candles.

"You gonna sit down again anytime soon?" he asked.

Mildred settled beside him. Her skirt flounced prettily about her, and she felt happy. "If I had a cookie mix I would make some more cookies for Fran and take them to her right now while she thinks she can eat them."

Jake stared at the lights on the Christmas tree. They were the kind he liked, all colors. They didn't blink either. They just glowed. It was the kind of Christmas lights that he had grown up with, and he liked them best of all.

"I have got a bag of the ladies' sugar cookies in the car. I forgot to bring them in. I will get them to Fran in the morning."

"You are coming back in the morning," she said, looking at the clock. It was after ten o'clock. She usually rose at five o'clock in order to have some time to pray before the day took hold.

"What time is breakfast?" he asked.

"Any time you get here," she said easily.

He grinned and kissed her lightly. And then he whispered in her ear.

"Me, too," she said, finally relaxing.

She leaned against him and closed her eyes. She felt safe with Jake Diamond. "Merry Christmas," she said.

"Isn't it?" he replied.

BONUS EXCERPT MILDRED BUDGE IN CLOVERDALE

Chapter 1

Visit from a Cereal Killer....

Retired school teacher Mildred Budge was standing naked in her laundry room remembering how her friend Cleo had died in the same state of undress, when she heard her front doorbell ring the first time. It couldn't be anyone she knew. All of Mildred Budge's friends knew to use the back door by the kitchen.

The timing was bad.

Mildred thought maybe she would just let whoever had come to the wrong house go away, when the doorbell rang again. And then, again. Insistently.

There was no ignoring it.

Only Mildred was naked, and everything she had been wearing while tagging dusty, mite-ridden furniture in the hot attic was now rotating inside the washing machine. On top of the clothes dryer were three lone unmatched black socks and one set of long underwear: white cotton Cuddl Duds that Mildred had intended to put away until the following winter.

As the bell rang five more times, Miss Budge decided that any clothes were better than none. Damp with perspiration and gritty with dust, she grabbed the Cuddl Duds and began the arduous task of wriggling into them. It wasn't easy. She looked down at herself in the clingy wintertime underwear that fit like a diaphanous white body stocking.

Victoria's Secret would not be hiring her pear-shaped frame to model lingerie.

"Miz Bulge! Are you all right in there?" A man's voice called out.

Her morning caller knew her, but she didn't recognize his voice. She heard the front doorknob jiggled impatiently. With a start, Miss Budge couldn't remember if she had locked the front door after bringing in the morning newspaper.

"I'm on my way!" Miss Budge called out, and her voice broke. Living alone with no one to talk to for long periods of time, one's voice became, occasionally, untrustworthy.

Tugging at the snug shirt that wanted to rise up and show her unpierced navel, Miss Budge hastily detoured to the foyer, pausing on the other side of her own front door to check the lock.

She peered through the peephole.

Miss Budge had never formally met her morning caller, but she did recognize him. Standing on her front door step was the young father who had moved with his wife and son into the old Garvin house across the street. The young man was wearing the same clothes she had always seen him in--faded black jeans and a black T-shirt. However, this was the first time the young father was close enough for Miss Budge to read the words stenciled on the front of the T-shirt: "Cereal Killer."

He was holding a large Ziploc bag with lumpy grains in it.

As she sent a news flash prayer to Jesus—'There's a cereal killer at my front door and I'm not fully dressed'—she called out, "Another moment, dear boy! I'll be right with you."

Miss Budge scooted to her bedroom and hurriedly slipped into her thick white chenille robe that she had bought for $19 at an after-Christmas sale three months ago. Adrenaline pumping, she clumsily pushed her still naked feet into sage green plastic Crocs. They were the ugliest shoes she had ever seen, but astonishingly comfortable.

"Miz Bulge! Is everything okay in there?" The Cereal Killer pounded on the door this time. Three hard raps.

Miss Budge cinched the thick robe firmly around her waist and scurried back to the front door, the toe of her right Crocs catching on the rug. She stumbled, and her arms batted the air as she fought to keep her footing. She got her balance back as the doorknob rattled again noisily.

"You haven't fallen or something, have you?" he called through the door.

Miss Budge wrenched the cold brassy doorknob and swung the front door open.

"Of course I have not fallen. Why would I?" Even as Miss Budge said the words, she remembered so many of her older friends for whom the end of their mobility was signaled by a commiserating tsk-tsk-tsk from every messenger who had ever delivered the dreaded news, "Oh, did you hear? She fell."

Cleo had fallen down naked in her laundry room and died alone. And she wasn't the only one of Mildred's acquaintances to begin that journey toward dependence on others in a hospital, nursing home, or assisted living with a fall.

Blinking at the mid-morning sunlight, Miss Budge offered a disciplined, cordial smile, one that had developed over twenty-five years of greeting scared fifth graders as a public school teacher and which had not diminished in the past two years since her retirement. "Young man, what is it you require so urgently?"

"Miz Bulge?" The Cereal Killer confirmed, squinting downward to meet her brown-eyed gaze. "You're shorter than they said."

"Why would people discuss my height?" Miss Budge inquired immediately, meeting his gaze unwaveringly, though she had to look up to do so. Her neighbor was tall and lanky with the kind of loose posture and untoned muscles that indicates a dearth of exercise.

"No. They said you was a great teacher, and somehow I jess thought you would be taller," he finished lamely. "I'm Kenny from across the street," he announced with a tip of his head toward the old Garvin house. "We been meaning to come say hi. The wife sent this to you," Kenny declared, holding out a gallon-size plastic Ziploc bag of what appeared to be rolled oats with raisins and slivered almonds.

Miss Budge reached politely for the proffered bag. Gifts of food usually came in covered white paper plates or disposable tin pans that she and her friends from the Berean Sunday school class chose to use when taking food to someone's house.

Miss Budge held the cellophane bag of grains up to the foyer light as if it were a bottle of special wine whose color she wanted to check. "How thoughtful," she murmured. "Won't you come in, Kenneth?"

"Thank you, Miz Bulge," Kenny said, stepping into her foyer. A heavy silver key chain slapped against his leg. He patted it companionably as if it were a small pet that was keeping him company. Squared bluish-black marks that reminded Miss Budge of some ancient Celtic designs set off his otherwise unmarred youthful hands.

When she peered more closely Miss Budge saw that the cribbed symbols were not a mysterious message in need of decoding but a single letter tattooed on each knuckle across the back of his hand that ultimately spelled out: L-O-V-E. Although she did not understand the allure of what amounted to inking graffiti upon one's person, Miss Budge, a spinster Christian lady, did believe in love. She smiled beneficently, as she adjusted the beige rheostat light switch in her expansive foyer.

The overhead light grew brighter, illuminating the various black and white photos on the wall of southern bridges that she had collected at one time in her life. Miss Budge had once upon a time loved the sight of aged bridges—loved the lines and arcs and the hope of them, shores being connected so people could cross over. But that season in her life had passed. The pictures were still hung, now a memorial to her previous affection for them rather than a celebration of the old-timey bridges themselves.

Kenny blinked rapidly, confused. She saw that Kenneth's eyes were a weak blue. Underneath the baseball cap that he did not take off, she assumed he was losing his hair prematurely.

"My last name is Budge. You have been calling me Miz Bulge," the retired teacher explained. She patted her mid-section. She was plumper than she had ever been. A frequent awareness of her increasing pear shape had not stopped the pounds from accruing, however. "But it's Mildred—Mildred Budge. Miss...." she declared forthrightly, unashamed of her singleness.

Kenny espied the pictures of solitary bridges on the walls. He blinked some more. The wispy, brown goatee on his chin waved gently when he spoke.

"Miz Deerborn told me about you."

"Will you sit down?" Miss Budge said, waving toward her living room. Her hands were bare of rings. She didn't wear jewelry when she had work to do, and she had spent a sticky morning in her hot attic tagging stored furniture that was to be taken and delivered to The Emporium, a local antique warehouse and flea market. She and her best friend Fran Applewhite were opening a sales booth.

Their initial inventory was the content of their respective attics: two lifetimes of acquired antiques (and a fair amount of old furniture) that would make them a fortune, predicted Fran-- or at least enough money so they could travel some.

"I won't stay long," Kenny promised, stepping carefully as if he didn't want to leave footprints on the glossy wooden floor. Kenneth's navy and white athletic shoes made the same small sticking sound against the taffy-colored hardwood floor as her green Crocs. As if mesmerized, her visitor revolved slowly, taking in the room before sitting down on the yellow chintz sofa and saying with wonder, "It's so clean in here."

Miss Budge automatically surveyed her living room, pausing to twist the clear plastic prismatic rod that opened her front mini-blinds. The room filled with sunlight. As the room grew brighter, Miss Budge saw that she needed to dust again. There was a small scrap of clipped white paper which must have escaped her paper shredder resting on the border of the large red and blue oriental carpet that defined the floor space. In a culture that necessarily lived with the threat of identity theft, Miss Budge had become a dedicated shredder of her monthly bills on which the numbers, if obtained, could facilitate the stealing of her credit cards, bank accounts, and most importantly, her identity. While shredding was yet another routine chore, Miss Budge liked doing it. She had invested in a sturdy stand-alone monster shredder from Costco that was stationed next to the telephone table, a superior style of furniture made sadly obsolete by cell phones.

Itching to pick up that errant scrap of white paper that disturbed her sense of order, Miss Budge said instead, "Kenneth, are you thirsty?" She had not lost that school teacherly tone. "Do you want a drink?" Her head bobbed up and down encouragingly. When she did, her brown curls caught the light, creating a halo effect that she would have enjoyed if she had known it was happening. She didn't.

"It's too early for me," Kenny said, sitting back on the sofa. "But you go ahead and take a drink if you need a little something.

I know how it is. I've got a granny who likes her wine in the morning, too."

Miss Budge's spine lengthened as her posture aligned itself with the truth.

"I do not need something to drink," she said, taken aback. Her forehead furrowed, deepening the lines that had grown from squinting while grading endless stacks of compositions written by students who did not have good penmanship. Miss Budge absent-mindedly massaged the tender place between her eyebrows that felt now like it retained some perpetual nerve damage. Then, she pressed her brown plastic eye glasses up on her nose; they slipped periodically. Soon, it would be time to go see Mr. Cates. He had been keeping her glasses adjusted for thirty years.

"Me and my wife moved in to that old house two months ago," Kenny said, with a jut of his whiskery chin toward the old Garvin house across the street.

Since Ron Garvin had died of some kind of dementia the legality of his last will had been questioned, and the potential heirs were fighting over his estate. The Garvin house was being rented out by the executor until the domicile could be legally sold and the profits distributed.

"Linda didn't want to live in Old Geezerville," Kenny explained, apparently unaware that the castigation of the Garden District in Montgomery, Alabama as Old Geezerville might be insulting to someone who had lived there her whole life.

The old geezers in reference were the long-time citizens of a southern city that had not only been the birthplace of the civil rights movement, but was also the home place of Zelda Fitzgerald, a famous belle and the wife of F. Scott. For those who cared, country singer Hank Williams was buried over at Oakwood Cemetery not too far from where Nathaniel Coles had lived when he was four years old with his family. In his teens he dropped the "s" and became Nat King Cole.

"I finally talked Baby into it. Our house is awesome. Really awesome, you know. We have what they call an attic fan. You can turn it on and open the windows. The air comes through just like the air conditioner was on," Kenny bragged. "It's going to save us a ton of money this summer, and it's already getting hotter by the day. We believe in going green." Kenny stared out at his own home through Miss Budge's front window and took a deep breath.

"Me and the wife make organic cereal. That's what I brought you right there. It'll get you going regular. That's our sales hook. These days, you either sell to people who can't sleep, can't lose weight, or to people who can't...." Kenny struggled for the word he needed, pressing his thin lips together, and finally settled on, "Who can't *go*. Cereal can't help you sleep," Kenny added lamely. "Although if that's all you ate, you probably could lose some weight."

There was an awkward pause.

Miss Budge could not discern Kenny's real purpose in coming to see her. Had he caught a glimpse of her and decided she needed to go on a diet?

Miss Budge was an unabashed size-14 woman, but fleshing out the seams of one's garments seemed to happen inevitably as one grew older. The better part of wisdom was to practice moderation in eating, walk as much as you could, and then accept your anatomy as it developed.

Miss Budge eyed the Cereal Killer with curiosity. It seemed unlikely to her that any newcomer would make it his personal mission to infiltrate an older neighborhood and then call on the plumper residents with the goal of putting them on a cereal diet in order to sell his product. Still, she could not recall a time in her life when anyone other than the doctor had ever brought up the subject of her regularity. She decided that the prudent course would be to change the subject.

"I know you are new to the neighborhood. It is actually referred to as Cloverdale—to some, Old Cloverdale," the retired school teacher explained patiently. When Kenny blinked as if he didn't speak English, she explained, "Cloverdale is considered to be the heart of historic Montgomery."

Kenny blinked some more, as if he didn't recognize the name of the city where they lived. Miss Budge smiled encouragingly, and continued politely. "I wonder if you have visited the Fitzgerald museum yet? It is to your left, about two miles that way," Miss Budge directed, pointing, and one more time, saw her mother's hand. She did not mind the vision of her mother's hand extending from her arm at all. Though no one expected a woman of Miss Budge's age to miss a parent, Mildred Budge still did miss her mother and was glad for the company of even the image of her mother's hand.

Kenny eyed the older woman as if she were speaking a foreign language. His eyes morphed to a weak shade of green. Miss Budge wondered if Kenneth was weak or just young. She had taught many young people and had learned that looking into their eyes and making assessments about intelligence or character based on an expression or shade of eye color had very little to do with who they really were—no more than how people once used to feel the bumps on a person's cranium to determine intelligence. Knowing that (and it had taken her a surprisingly long time to learn it) Miss Budge often fought the impulse anyway to a know person's head shape with her fingertips, like a blind person might. Kenny had a rectangular-shaped head. Her fingers began to strum the air gently. If she could know the contours of his head with her hands, what would the arcs and bumps tell her about what was going on inside? She clasped her hands determinedly in her lap and held them there while surreptitiously checking the closure of her robe.

Her mother would have liked this robe, too, she thought—and smiled.

"The museum is the old house of a famous Montgomery family. F. Scott Fitzgerald is a famous author. He married a Montgomery girl," she explained patiently. "You may recall from your high school days that Fitzgerald wrote *The Great Gatsby*."

Kenny stared at Miss Budge blankly, and the color of his eyes deepened to the color of an ocean just before it rained. Troubled, Kenny tried to figure out what to say next.

When he didn't immediately speak, Miss Budge continued. "His wife Zelda Sayre was not only a famous southern belle here but a talented writer as well."

Kenny's fingertips scratched the tops of his thighs as if he were getting ready to explain the purpose of his visit. Miss Budge nodded encouragingly, but Kenny did not respond to her cue.

"Or, there's Martin Luther King, Jr.'s church downtown or The First White House of the Confederacy," she added, sounding like one of those volunteer tour guides that some senior citizens become to fill their days after they retired. Though she was retired—prematurely, according to some—she was still too busy to volunteer in that capacity.

Kenny blinked and said, "Awesome." He rubbed his palms on the tops of his jeans. The silver chain with the keys jangled. He petted it.

Miss Budge felt impatient then, though she hid it. Fran and Winston were coming over with the truck in a half hour, and she needed to shower and dress before they arrived. Certainly, the delivery of cereal could not have been Kenneth's primary goal. "Are you sure you don't want some lemonade?" his hostess prompted. She could get it, he could drink it, he could leave.

Kenny shook his head, no, looking as if he might rise. But he didn't. "Miz Bulge...."

Determined to be polite, Miss Budge sat back in the uncomfortable turquoise chair. She had forgotten how unforgiving the chair was. Miss Budge shifted her derriere, struggling for a different center of gravity that might ease the rigidity, but she did not find it.

"Miz Bulge," Kenny said, beginning again, his gaze drifting around the room. "I been watching your house, and you go to church on Sundays. You carry a Bible and everything," Kenny declared. And his nervous hands came to a rest on the tops of his thighs, as he looked to his right at the table with the reading lamp. There were three different Bibles on it.

Kenny's eyes caught hers, and he pressed on. "My son is not a friendly boy. It's like he's not even there sometimes, you know? He's seven. He's supposed to be in school; but Baby---Linda, my wife---thinks Chase won't fit in at school because of his not talking. She's been trying to home school him, but it ain't going as well as she hoped it would. Baby's not a teacher, don't you see?" Kenny said, and his tattooed fingers began to strum the tops of his black-denimed thighs again, spelling out L-O-V-E over and over again.

Miss Budge nodded almost imperceptibly, and the warmth in her brown eyes faded to a wary watchfulness.

"You being a schoolteacher and all..."

Mildred assumed the 'and all' referred to going to church on Sunday and carrying a Bible.

"And I hear you still go to houses of sick kids sometimes...."

"Not anymore," Mildred replied carefully. Initially, after her sudden decision to retire two years ago--and because she needed the money to supplement her reduced fixed income--Miss Budge had accepted short-term assignments as a teacher for homebound students.

But she hadn't done that work for long. The children were too sick and too brave, and they had asked Miss Budge questions that were too hard to answer. She knew the answers; she just didn't want to say them out loud to young children in pain.

Kenny slapped the tops of his black jeans and finally got to his point. "I was wondering if you could help my boy."

"I am not a doctor," Mildred Budge replied, postponing the polite but firm 'no' she would offer Kenny in a moment just as soon as she framed it in her mind. She had left that kind of work

201

behind--cried as many tears as she could. Besides, it was never wise to get caught up in the neighbors' domestic problems, especially if they lived as close as across the street. Before she could say no, her telephone rang.

Loudly.

Miss Budge had only one phone, and she kept the ringer on 'Loud' so that she could hear it ring anywhere in the house. She always answered her phone calls beside her wooden telephone table where a writing tablet and pen were readily available for note-taking and where the small seat built into the table gave her a place to rest in case the caller was long-winded. She sat there to do her monthly shredding, too. Other people thought that speaking on the telephone or shredding the monthly bills were tasks that happened in concert with other activities; it was called multitasking. But Mildred Budge did not like splitting her attention; she liked being focused, had learned as a school teacher that giving one's attention to a person or a job resulted in a better understanding of that person and a better job when work was to be done.

Kenny waited for Miss Budge to move and answer the telephone. She did not.

"I don't answer the telephone when I have a guest," Miss Budge explained simply as the ringing continued, then stopped abruptly.

Kenny laughed. Genuinely. As if the explanation of good manners was some kind of joke. "Miz Deerborn said you was funny and for me not to be afraid of you."

Ah, Belle Deerborn. The well-intentioned woman—and a good friend, too-- who lived just behind Mildred Budge on the other side of the circle that connected their intersecting yards.

Kenneth leaned forward and said in what was almost a whisper: "Miz Belle said you have the gift of healing kids."

Immediately, Miss Budge began to shake her head, no. "I was a teacher. That is all," she replied firmly. "You are wrong—and so is Belle—if you think otherwise."

"Miz Deerborn said you would say that," Kenny replied immediately, his brown wispy goatee wagging.

"It is the truth," Miss Budge replied unswervingly. "I do not glamorize the fruits of determined work by calling it something it is not."

Kenneth nodded as if he were in on the conspiracy of discretion that Miss Budge was determined to perpetuate. "Maybe you could jess speak to my boy then," he said with a wink. "Jest your speaking to him would be good, 'cause Chase don't talk to nobody, even us, sometimes." Kenny took an anxious breath and switched tactics, attempting to persuade her. "That cereal I brought you is all organic. 'S very good for you. No chemicals, pesticides, etcetera, etcetera, etcetera. Let me know if you like it, and I'll bring you a bunch more." Kenny stood up then suddenly. He had finished the job he had given himself to do. The sun shifted from behind a cloud and spilled fresh illumination into the room right where he was standing. The angles of his square-shaped head were easily discerned as bumps inside the baseball cap he had never removed. Miss Budge read his mind then: he had come to see the lady across the street, brought her his offering, made his request, and now he was going home.

Miss Budge was ready for him to go, and she stood more slowly, not because she was older or creaky or less able to stand, but because in her generation one did not rush others out the door by rising too quickly. There was always a hint in every gesture that parting was sweet sorrow—really.

Miss Budge smiled as she followed him to the foyer, speaking in the pace of having an infinite amount of time to get to know other people that others erroneously and inappropriately judged harshly as an irritating habit of an older person, but it was only courtesy. "That explains why the UPS truck comes to your house so often. He must be bringing you supplies for your organic cereals," she theorized aloud, as Kenny led the way to her front door.

Kenny's voice grew proud. "We sell on the internet a lot, and we take it over to the health food store on the Easter by-pass. We have mucho customers now," Kenny said proudly, as her telephone began to ring again. "Somebody really wants to talk to you," Kenny said. "I'll go on and get out of your way."

He turned in the doorway and said, his voice growing quieter: "My boy's name is Chase, and you don't know him yet, but he's special."

Miss Budge met the young father's gaze, so similar to the faces of so many young parents of young children who had been in her care during the twenty-five years she had served the state in the public school system. Kenny was a stranger, but Miss Budge knew him. Kenny was a young father who had a son who was special.

"You could come over any time. Any time at all that suits you. Linda would love to meet you," Kenny promised, looking across the street to his new home where the blinds were closed, and no lights appeared to be on inside. There was something in that anxious glance at his own home that moved Miss Budge. She relented.

"I'd be delighted to meet your Chase," Mildred agreed, casting an involuntary glance at the insistent telephone as it continued to ring.

Kenneth fired an imaginary pistol at her with his forefinger and thumb, and Miss Budge marveled at a hand gesture that spoke of a violence that was inconsonant with the nature of his request. Still, she fought the urge born of politeness to mimic Kenneth's hand movement, offering a short wave of farewell instead as she walked toward the telephone. On the way, Mildred stooped over and picked up the scrap of white paper that had been bothering her. It was a piece of notebook paper, not a piece of a shredded bill.

"Greetings to you and yours," Miss Budge said, answering the phone.

"Have you been drinking?" Fran Applewhite asked sharply.

Before Mildred could answer, Fran said, "That was me calling before; but then I thought you might be in the attic, and if I let it keep ringing, you might break your neck trying to answer the telephone. You don't want to die in the attic. It would have been hard as all get-out to bring your body down those stairs. Remember how hard it was to get the broken water heater down? So I hung up and waited a spell. I have news. It's big," Fran warned.

"I was not in the attic. I was in my living room talking with a cereal killer who thinks that the Eastern by-pass is named after Easter Sunday or the Easter bunny. It is unclear which one he has in mind."

Fran interrupted her. "Mildred, she's killed another one."

Mildred didn't have to ask who Fran meant. She knew. Liz Luckie had recently married for the fourth time; and each time, the husbands had died early in the marriage. Mildred had not known the first three husbands, but she had been a special friend of Liz's most recent groom.

"How did Hugh die?" Mildred asked. She sat down heavily in the small seat built into the telephone table. It was a tight fit. It didn't use to be.

"The regular way. Natural causes." Fran reported bluntly.

"Natural causes. Again," Mildred repeated bleakly. She patted her face with one hand. She felt pale. Then, she pressed the same hand to her chest. Her heart was beating fast. The chenille robe was thick. She was wearing long underwear, too, but Mildred felt chilled. Her lower lip trembled. No hot flash conveniently arrived when it might have helped to warm her.

"They all die of natural causes," Fran said quietly. She hesitated before adding, "Today's Thursday. I figure the funeral will be Saturday."

Mildred nodded into the telephone, her throat instantly dry. Yes. That might be hard for someone else to arrange, but for a woman who had already orchestrated three funerals for her previous husbands, arranging a funeral in two days would not be a problem. She wouldn't have the funeral on a Sunday afternoon, and Monday was too late.

"I wanted to tell you before Winston and I got there together with his truck because that's not the kind of news you need to hear in front of company," Fran explained, her voice dropping to a whisper.

Winston must have come inside Fran's house and was now standing near enough to Fran to hear what she was trying to tell Mildred quietly.

Mildred swallowed hard, remembering how before Hugh had married Liz, his fingertips had grazed hers in the church kitchen when he had handed her his water glass to be washed on a Saturday morning. Each had volunteered to participate in the deep spring cleaning of the church building.

And before that, Hugh had sat beside her in Sunday school as if he just happened to land there and how nervous his sitting close had made her feel—and crowded.

And Hugh had asked her to dance after one of the church weddings at the country club, and she hadn't said no fast enough. Hugh had taken her in his arms and steered her around, and while they moved—scuttled crablike is how Mildred described it to herself—about the floor, she had endured an embarrassing hot flash and broken out in a flop sweat of sorts that Hugh didn't seem to notice, but, of course, he had noticed.

"I've got to go now, Millie. It'll be all right," Fran whispered before hanging up. Mildred's best friend said the words with the authority of a veteran widow who had told herself the same thing through many a long night spent without Gritz who had died on her—the husband Fran Applewhite had loved dearly for forty-three years.

BOOKS BY DAPHNE SIMPKINS

The Mildred Budge novels

Mildred Budge in Cloverdale (book 1)

Mildred Budge in Embankment (book 2)

The Bride's Room (book 3)

Kingdom Come (book 4)

The Fort (coming next, book 5)

The Mildred Budge shorter stories and novella

Miss Budge in Love (short story collection, book 1)

The Mission of Mildred Budge (short story collection, book 2)

Miss Budge Goes to Fountain City (book 3 a novella)

A Mildred Budge Friendship Story

Belle: A Mildred Budge Friendship Story (book 1)

A Gentle and Lowly Christmas (book 2)

Stand-alone Fiction

Lovejoy: a novel about desire

Christmas in Fountain City (a cross-over prequel to Miss Budge Goes to Fountain City)

Tricks of the Mind

Essays and Non-fiction

What Makes a Man a Hero? Stories about men for Father's Day

A Cookbook for Katie Recipes and Reveries for the Bride

Blessed Stories about Caregiving

What Al Left Behind Essays about Caregiving

The Long Good Night a memoir about caregiving

ABOUT DAPHNE SIMPKINS

Daphne Simpkins is an Alabama writer best known for the Mildred Budge stories. She has also written about caregiving and other aspects of daily life. Follow her on Amazon, Facebook, or BookBub. Contact her through: QuotidianToday@gmail.com

Made in the USA
Monee, IL
03 October 2024

67095557R00118